Yael AND THE Party OF THE Year

ALSO BY TAMSIN LANE

Tara Takes the Stage

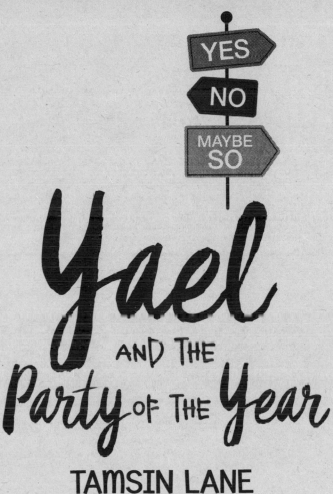

YES
NO
MAYBE
SO

Yael

AND THE

Party OF THE Year

TAMSIN LANE

SIMON & SCHUSTER CANADA

NEW YORK LONDON TORONTO SYDNEY NEW DELHI

SIMON & SCHUSTER CANADA

A Division of Simon & Schuster, Inc.

166 King Street East, Suite 300

Toronto, Ontario M5A 1J3

This book is a work of fiction. Any references to historical events, real people,
or real places are used fictitiously. Other names, characters, places, and events are products of
the author's imagination, and any resemblance to actual events or places
or persons, living or dead, is entirely coincidental.

Text by Joanne Levy

Book design by Alicia Mikles

The text for this book was set in Lomba.

Manufactured in the United States of America

1221 OFF

This PJ Our Way edition ©2019

ISBN 978-1-921-2383-3

How to read a
Yes No Maybe So book.

As you read, you will come across a set of choices. Turn to the page shown and continue reading until your next set of choices. When you get to the end, you can start all over again!

Yael and the Party of the Year

Artistic Differences

"Shoe hurts! MAMA! SHOE HURTS!"

Well, I had to give Rivka—my two-and-a-half-year-old sister—credit: Her reasons for having full-on, wailing, red-faced, and inconsolable tantrums were always random, creative, *and* varied.

But it didn't matter what she was going on about this time; that it was embarrassing and annoying *never* changed.

Slowly and inconspicuously I sidestepped away from the scene: her lying on her back, flailing her arms and legs in the middle of the Temple Shalom parking lot. I aimed for the colorful bush that hadn't yet lost all its leaves. The plan was to hide behind it until Ranting Rivka got herself under control. It was so humiliating that she was related to me; I hated drama more than anything.

My parents looked flustered as they stood there, desperately trying to calm her down (I don't know why they bothered—it *never* worked) while people heading toward the synagogue shook their heads. I could imagine the scene as a painting—a slice-of-life tableau entitled *Mortification*.

I almost felt bad for Mom and Dad. *Almost.* I mean, they were the reason she existed, right? I felt it hard to be too sympathetic when you created your own problem.

"Hey, Yael," came a voice from just behind me.

I eagerly pivoted away from my embarrassing family to greet the friendly voice and was happy to see Eli Roth. Eli was not only my next-door neighbor but was also in my bar and bat mitzvah class. We'd practiced our Torah portions together until his bar mitzvah at the beginning of the summer.

He'd been away for the last month, and though we'd been back at school for a week already, we had somehow missed each other in the chaos. I suddenly realized that I hadn't seen him in a long time.

He was very tanned, and his sandy-brown hair had blond highlights from the summer sun. Both changes made his blue eyes seem even bluer.

"Hey, Eli," I said, pushing my glasses up my nose. "It's been forever since I've seen you! How was your summer?"

He shrugged. "It was okay. The camper van was pretty cramped with the five of us."

"Right," I said, remembering that his parents, who weren't great at planning, had decided at the last minute to take the family in a rented RV and tour around the country, visiting national parks and probably not bathing very often. Not my idea of a fun summer. Nor Eli's, it would seem.

"Oh, that sounds . . . interesting," I said, trying to be nice.

He laughed. "Parts of it were okay, like being able to see way more stars when driving through the countryside," he said before his face twisted into a frown. "After my bar mitzvah I was glad to get out of town for a while. Although I would have preferred camp or somewhere that my parents weren't, if you know what I mean."

I nodded sympathetically. I *did* know what he meant. His bar mitzvah had been a complete and total disaster.

Eli had wanted to have a huge pool party to kick off the summer, one that all the kids would remember. But it was scheduled for the first long weekend of the summer, *and* his flaky parents forgot to send out invites until the last minute. It was—well, I hate to say it—a bust. A *major* bust.

He'd done an okay job with his Torah reading at the service, performing to the small crowd in the synagogue. But after that it went downhill. What was supposed to be a huge party for more than a hundred people was barely a cringe-worthy two dozen—and that included mostly his family and grandparents.

After the service we'd gathered at the Knot's Valley Community Center, but soon after we arrived, it began to thunder. Lightning flashed. And then there was hail. The giant balls of ice didn't just splash into the pool, either. They came down over the whole deck, popping the balloons. We watched helplessly from inside the center as hail crashed down on the buffet table.

To say the food—including the beautiful tiered cake—was ruined was a giant understatement. It had been obliterated.

When Eli's dad laughed and said that with so few guests a pizza bill wouldn't be too big, well, I thought Eli was going to have a Ranting Rivka–type of meltdown.

I hardly would have blamed him. It was definitely a party we'd all remember. But not in a good way.

Which was why *I* was having a small family-and-friends-only dinner to celebrate my bat mitzvah. The last thing I needed was that kind of drama. Or rather, *trauma*.

"How about your bat mitzvah?" Eli asked, as though he were reading my mind. Just then my sister let out a long and loud howl behind me. Eli's wide eyes darted over my shoulder at what sounded like a crime in progress. "Is that Rivka?" he asked, his alarmed gaze returning to mine.

I adjusted my glasses and sighed, not needing to turn around to confirm it. "Yes. This is sort of her thing now," I said with a dismissive wave of my hand. It was amazing how I'd ever thought Rivka was cute. "Anyway, about my bat mitzvah . . ." I was cut off by an eardrum-bursting screech that I did my best to ignore, but it was getting harder.

Finally, when there was a moment of silence, I opened my mouth, but Eli asked, "Do you have your Torah portion nailed yet?"

I thought about my bat mitzvah. The Jewish

ceremony signifies a person becoming an adult and being responsible for their own actions, but first that person has to sing part of the Torah.

On a stage.

In front of the entire synagogue congregation. In Hebrew.

Singing. On a *stage*. To a *zillion people*. In *Hebrew*.

This wouldn't have been an issue for my best friend, Tara Singh, who was a natural performer and loved the spotlight on her at all times. But for me, who preferred to paint and was not a very good singer, it was a tiny bit terrifying. And by a tiny bit, I mean colossally.

"Uh, not exactly," I said, nerves rattling my chest, because while I knew all the words and could sing along with the recording that the rabbi had e-mailed, it was one thing to practice in the mirror and another to recite it in front of a million people.

"Oh," Eli said. "Well, if you want to come over, I can help you practice. It is kind of a big deal, so . . ."

I opened my mouth to answer, when I heard, "What's a big deal?"

I looked behind me, and there was my mom

with a smiling but red-eyed Rivka in her arms, perched on her hip. So weird how my sister could be freaking out one minute and the happiest kid in the world the next.

"Yael's bat mitzvah is a big deal," Eli said.

"Of course it is!" Mom exclaimed, leaning into me. "We couldn't be more excited, right, Yael?"

"So excited!" Rivka shouted, mimicking Mom's enthusiasm. I wouldn't admit it out loud, but okay, sometimes the kid was kind of cute. Her brown hair was like mine, but hers was in ringlets, and that, paired with her pale, chubby cheeks, made her look like an adorable little angel. Not that she acted like one most of the time.

"Sure," I said. "I mean, I love Dumplings."

Mom looked from me to Eli and then back again. "Dumplings?"

"Uh, yeah, Dumplings," I said. "My favorite restaurant. The one where we're going to have my bat mitzvah dinner? With you guys and the grandparents and a few of my friends."

Mom frowned. "Noooooo," she said, stretching out the word. "That's not what we're doing."

I blinked at her several times before I said, "But . . . I thought . . ."

Mom shook her head as she interrupted me.

"Yael, we are not having your bat mitzvah at a *restaurant*." She said the word "restaurant" as though she were saying "the dump." I frowned as she continued. "This is a very big deal, a once-in-a-lifetime event. We are having a party. A *big* party. Everyone will be invited to share your special day."

"No," I said, my heart pounding in my chest. "I don't want a big party. I don't want the . . ." I was about to say "trauma," but I saw Eli fidgeting out of the corner of my eye. "I'm nervous enough about performing my Torah portion. I don't need a party where I have to make a speech and be on display. I don't want the attention," I added. It was the truth, if not the whole truth.

"Don't be silly," Mom said, shifting Rivka to her other hip. "Of course you want the attention. That's what being a bat mitzvah is all about. We're celebrating *your* entry into adulthood. This is all about *you*."

"All about you!" Rivka announced.

Seriously, kid? I was starting to sweat, and not from the heat.

"But I don't want that," I said. "Save the money. We'll just have a small dinner. Just us. And a few of my friends."

Mom shook her head. "It's not about the money. We want to do this for you. We want everyone to see how wonderful you are. How proud we are of you."

"But I don't want that," I repeated, starting to sound whiny, but when I glanced over at Eli, he'd disappeared. Just as well, I guess; this conversation was embarrassing. And I feared it was only going to get worse.

"Yael," my mother said in a very stern tone. "You are having a bat mitzvah party, and you are going to enjoy yourself! You'll see; it will be the best bat mitzvah ever!"

Really? I squinted at her. Did she realize how ridiculous she sounded? She just smiled at me cluelessly, so I guess not.

"Best bat mitzvah evah!" Rivka exclaimed.

I looked at my suddenly sweet sister and tried not to scream in frustration. Thirteen years old was definitely too old to throw a tantrum. Luckily, I wasn't thirteen yet. I stormed into the synagogue.

Sketching It Out

Shabbat was finally over, and that meant I could have my phone back. In my house the day of rest meant taking a break from electronics, which could be annoying, especially when I absolutely needed to talk to Tara.

"Ugh," I growled into the phone. "They are being TOTALLY UNREASONABLE!"

"Ugh," Tara echoed, and I could picture her shaking her head in sympathy.

"I can't believe they are *making* me have a party! If having a bat mitzvah means I'm going to be an adult, why can't they treat me like one and let me do what *I* want to do?"

"That is *the worst*," Tara said quickly. But after a long pause she added, "Buuuuuut . . ." Her voice trailed off.

"What?" What could she possibly be adding a "but" about?

"I just . . . I'm not sure I understand the *actual* problem."

"Are you kidding me right now, Tara?" She always had my back, but we could sometimes be as different as latkes and dosas.

"Don't get mad, but"—there was that "but" again—"a big party sounds amazing, don't you think?"

"No, I do not think!" I shrieked, sounding remarkably like Rivka.

I took a deep breath and looked up at the ceiling. I forced myself to use a calm voice when I spoke again. "No. A party *doesn't* sound amazing. I don't want it. I just want this all to be over. The Torah reading, the adulting, the . . . all of it."

"But, Yael, this is all *for you*. This is a VBD! Why wouldn't you want a party where you're the center of attention?!"

I blew out a loud sigh. I knew this was a Very Big Deal, which is why I wanted *only* my best friends and family with me to celebrate, not all of Knot's Valley. "Tara, *you* like being the center of attention. *I* don't. I would rather go to *your* bat mitzvah as a guest than have my own."

That made her laugh. "Maybe I should have one! A Bollywood bat mitzvah!"

I giggled. "If only! You're practically Jewish!" Tara laughed too. Most people I knew pronounced it phonetically—like the flying rodent—but as my lifelong friend, she knew to say "bot mitzvah."

"Yael," Tara said, sounding earnest. "I really want to celebrate with you. And I'm sure your parents do too."

"It's not like I have a choice," I muttered.

"Stop being so negative," she admonished. "You'll see—it will be the party of the year!"

I pressed my lips together while she went on. "What does your mom have planned, anyway?"

I thought back to the giant fight I'd had with my parents. The one that started on the way home from shul and lasted until I'd stormed off to my room to cool down. At dinner Dad called a time-out on it so we could eat (which we did in tense silence), but after doing the dishes and more arguing, my tired parents finally gave me my phone back since Shabbat was over. That's when

I immediately stomped up to my room and called Tara.

"They—or should I say, *my mother*—want to have a boring hotel party, where everyone dresses up and eats finger food and listens to old-person music or whatever."

"Ooooh, sounds so fancy!" Tara said in a wistful voice. "Except the old-person music, obvs."

"Not helping, Tara!" I exclaimed. "She also wants to invite the entire planet. Not just my entire family, but both eighth-grade classes, too!"

"Oh, all your friends there to celebrate your special day. How *horrible* for you, Yael!"

Tara Singh, star of stage and sarcasm.

I let out a big sigh, and she responded with a dramatic groan. "Don't you *want* to get dressed up and dance? That sounds like a great time."

"Tara, I just want you and Gemma and Paloma there. Maaaaayybe some kids from my bar and bat mitzvah class. But that's it." I paused. "If I have to have any sort of party, I want something fun we can all do together. I don't want to be on display, you know? It's bad enough that I have to be onstage during the synagogue part."

"I guess," my best friend said, but I knew she didn't really get it.

I wasn't sure what to say after that, but then she said, "Hey, wait a minute. If your mom is inviting *all* eighth graders, that means Cam Thompson will be there too!"

"Oh" was all I said to that, but my brain started whirling. I had been so wrapped up in my nervousness about my performance and the party that it had never occurred to me that Cameron Thompson—the cute guy I was totally crushing on—might be there. Except, would he even *want* to go to my bat mitzvah? Especially a boring one at a stuffy old hotel?

I looked out my window and noticed Eli in his backyard next door. As an astrophysicist wannabe, he spent a lot of time outside at night. One night last summer we'd sat in his yard, and he'd pointed out all the stars. I was impressed he knew all the constellations and had gone home to draw him a picture of the night sky—I'd even checked online to make sure I got all the stars right. He'd told me he loved it so much that he tacked it to the ceiling above his bed.

As I watched him now, he was gently swinging side to side in his hammock, the glow of his tablet lighting up his face, looking oh so relaxed. I felt a pang of jealousy, because even though his bar mitzvah had been a disaster, at least it was *over*. I couldn't wait until *I* could finally feel that relaxed.

"Yael? You there?" Tara's voice broke into my thoughts.

"Yeah, yeah, of course, sorry. I was just thinking."

"About?"

"Tara, you *know* me. I do *not* want a hotel party."

"Weeeeelllllllll . . ."

"What?" I asked, because I recognized her "I have an idea" tone. I both loved and was afraid of that tone.

"Does it *have* to be at a hotel?" she asked. "Is it some sort of Jewish law?"

I laughed. "No. At least I've never read anything about bat mitzvah parties being held at hotels in the Torah. I think that's just where my mom wants to hold it because it's classy."

"So if it doesn't really matter, maybe *you* can pick where the party is. If your parents just want the big party, shouldn't *you* get to choose the location? That sounds like a pretty good compromise to me."

I turned away from the window, loving my best

friend so much right then. "You know, that sounds like a pretty good compromise to me, too, Tara."

"Aaaaaaand if you get to choose, shouldn't you choose somewhere fun?"

"I like how you think, Tara, but where . . ."

Then, like we shared a brain, we both blurted out: "The Maize!"

The Maize. I fell asleep thinking about the old-timey amusement park that had been renovated in the spring. Tara and I had been waiting all summer to visit, but between my going to camp and Tara working at her family's sweet shop, we hadn't had a chance to check it out yet. Our other friends had gone on and on about the updated rides, midway games, the crazy corn maze, and, of course, the carnival food. I knew it would be the perfect place for my bat mitzvah party.

"You can't have a bat mitzvah at an amusement park," my mother said incredulously the next morning, as though I'd suggested we have the party on Mars. Although Mars would be better than a boring hotel. At least Eli would have a good time.

"Did you hear her, Simon?" she demanded of my father.

"I did, and . . ." He looked at me and winked before he turned back to her. "I think it's a good idea."

My heart leaped. He was definitely my favorite parent at that moment.

"WHAT?" Mom yelled.

"Becky. Think about it. Yael makes a good point about wanting to be treated like an adult. I think we should respect her, and if that's where she wants to have her party—not the actual Torah reading, because obviously that will take place at shul on a Saturday morning, right?" He looked at me to confirm, and when I nodded, he went on. "Then I think it's a great idea."

"But I—"

Dad cut her off with a shake of his head. "It's not about you, Becky. It's about our daughter. And how about this: On the Saturday we'll have a nice kiddush brunch in the hall at the synagogue after the service, and then the next day we can have the fun party at the Maize. It's a long weekend, so no one has to go to school or work that Monday, and we can make it a whole weekend extravaganza."

I couldn't help beaming at Dad's idea—it was perfect! And he was selling it well to Mom. If *anyone* loved an *extravaganza*, it was her.

Mom huffed, but when Dad gave me another wink, I knew it meant we had her.

Could this maybe happen? I didn't dare hope. Except I did. I hoped *hard*.

Without a word, she grabbed her phone and started tapping at the screen. I looked at Dad, but he just shrugged. We both faced Mom to see how this was going to play out.

She then brought the phone to her ear and, a few seconds later, began to speak.

"Hello? I was wondering if I could be put in touch with whoever handles your events. . . . Yes, I'll hold." Mom looked at me and shook her head.

What did this mean? Who was she calling?

A moment later her spine straightened and she nodded. "Yes, that's right. I need to book a party. A bat mitzvah. Yes, I know you're an amusement park, but my daughter wants to have her party at the Maize, and she's almost an adult, so . . ."

A squeal escaped my lips as I jumped to hug my dad.

I couldn't wait to start planning!

A Motif

Monday morning came too soon. It was my own fault for staying up so late, but still, I was annoyed at my mother for not letting me sleep in. She didn't even seem to care that the reason I'd stayed up was to prepare for my bat mitzvah.

After I had a shower, cleaned my glasses, did my hair, and downed some breakfast, I felt a little better. And then, when I remembered that my party was going to be at the Maize, I felt *a lot* better.

Especially as I looked down at the hand-painted invitations I'd stayed up late to design. They'd turned out so well.

Mom had taken me to the craft store so I could get thick, creamy paper; paints; and some new oil-painting pens.

Back in my room I got to work, carefully folding each paper crosswise. On the front of some of the cards I drew the lines of a Ferris wheel in the blackest ink. On other cards I outlined a barn, and on the rest I drew a corn maze. My hands were covered in ink by the time I was done, but I made sure to be careful and not smudge—I needed to keep the cards pristine. As I waited for them all to dry, I looked over the array of invitations spread across my desk, smiling at the bold designs.

Now to channel my inner Maud Lewis, I thought. I loved that I shared a last name with one of my favorite artists, and I liked to think that I shared her vision with color.

Once the ink was dry, I got out my paints and added a few tiny details in color to make each invitation unique. Inside the cards, on the bottom half, I penned the date and location of the actual bat mitzvah event at the synagogue on the Saturday, and then the details of the Sunday party at the Maize. Below, I added my phone number in fall colors and a folksy style.

I looked at it for a long minute because it still felt like it needed something. *Yael's bat mitzvah.* BOT mitzvah. Inspiration hit me like a splatter of paint!

Above the fold I scrawled *YAEL'S BAT* and painted a silver robot wearing glasses that looked like mine. I added freckles and examined my work. I snorted. Robot Yael was pretty cheeky.

Leaving a bunch for my parents to send out to family, I made two bundles of invites to take to school to give out, but I needed someone to help me distribute them to the rest of the eighth graders.

Tara and Gemma were in my homeroom, which left Paloma, but I wouldn't see her until lunch. I wanted to pass out the invitations first thing.

I left the house to walk to Tara's, my backpack over my shoulders and the box of invitations in my hands, when the answer hit me.

Literally.

"Look out!" Eli yelled, but way too late. The second I heard his voice and turned, I was beaned in the head by a soccer ball, my glasses flying off my face as I dropped the box.

"Noooooo!"

Luckily, the box stayed closed, and nothing fell out when it hit the ground. My hand rose to rub the spot, just above my ear, where I'd been hit.

"Sorry!" Eli and his little brother, Stevie, yelled out at the same time.

"You guys!" I yelled, but I wasn't mad. I'd been surprised, not hurt. I reached for my glasses, which thankfully were not broken, and shoved them onto my face.

"Sorry," Eli said again, reddening as he neared.

That's when I remembered that Eli was in the other eighth-grade class.

"It's okay," I said, still rubbing my head. "No permanent damage. But I'm pretty sure this means you owe me a favor."

"Of course!" Eli said in a guilty voice as he nodded. But then he stopped and looked at me sideways. "Wait, what kind of favor?"

I picked up the box and showed him the cards. "I made these last night. Can you hand some out to everyone in your class?"

He leaned over to look at the invitations. My very favorite—one of a Ferris wheel with thirteen sparkly gold cars was right on top. I'd used a special glitter paint to make the cars really pop, and it had turned out perfectly, especially as I looked at it now, glinting in the sunlight.

"Hey, those are awesome," Eli said, his eyes darting up to mine. "Did you make them all?"

I beamed. All that lost sleep suddenly felt worth it. "Thanks. And yeah, I made them all myself."

"Whoa, those are cool," Stevie said as he reached into the box. Before he could grab one with his grubby hands, I pulled the box back.

"You'll get one," I said. "But these are for the eighth graders."

Stevie made a face.

"Sure, I'll take them," Eli said. "Which pile?"

I held out a bundle.

"For sure." He wiped his palms on his jeans—which I appreciated—and then reached for the stack of invites.

As he took them, I had an idea. "Hey, so that one on the top? That one's for Cam."

"Oh," Eli said, looking down at the invites in his hands. "Are everyone's names on them?"

"Uh, no, just . . . um, that one is for him. The rest can go to anyone." My face heated up, but I wasn't going to explain to Eli that I wanted Cam to have the best invitation.

I felt Eli's eyes on me, but I was looking down at my shoes, avoiding his gaze.

"Which one do I get?" he asked.

I lifted my eyes and saw a weird, sort of hopeful look on his face. I glanced at the other pile that was for my own class. The card on top was pretty with thirteen gold stars and the moon painted on it. That fit, since Eli was into planets and space things.

I pulled it out and handed it to him. "This one," I said.

"Yeah?" he said, his voice full of awe, like I really had made it just for him.

I nodded.

"Cool, thanks!"

"You're welcome," I said, noticing he still looked awfully red. Maybe he was hot from kicking around the soccer ball.

But he was also staring at me oddly. "What?" I said with a frown, sure that my freckles were beet red. How had this conversation gotten so awkward so quickly?

"I'm looking forward to your bat mitzvah," he said in a weird voice as he stared right into my eyes.

Okaaaaaay. "Great. Thanks."

"Why don't you come over this Friday after school, and I can help you practice? My brothers are staying over at my grandparents, so they won't bug us."

I looked at Eli, my oldest friend and next-door neighbor. He looked different after the summer away. Was that possible after only a few weeks?

He stared at me, waiting for an answer. "Maybe," I said quickly. "Anyway, thanks so much for handing those out."

He nodded. "Of course, yeah."

"Um, I have to go meet Tara. Don't forget to give that top one to Cam," I said, glancing at my wrist as though I were wearing a watch (I wasn't). "Shoot, I'm late now. I'd better run!"

And then I did.

"These invitations are ADORABLE. I love how they're all a little different!" Gemma exclaimed, beaming at the cards then at me then back at the cards, her black curls bouncing.

We were in the cafeteria later that day at lunch. It was the four of us as usual: Paloma, Gemma beside her, and across from them, Tara and me. We'd finished eating, and Gemma, who could be a little bossy sometimes, had made sure everyone's hands were clean before they passed around their three invitations.

I'd felt a little nervous to share the invites because they were handmade and not as fancy as some of the ones that I'd received from other kids in my bar and bat mitzvah class. But then, when my classmates all seemed to like them—comparing them to see all the little differences—I was glad I had done it my way.

"You are *so* talented," Paloma said. Her almond-shaped eyes flicked from the invites to me and then back again. "I'm going to frame mine and put it on my wall beside the photo of my top score in Minecraft."

"Next to gaming stuff? Really?" Tara said, holding up her invitation, the one I'd painted with red and blue bumper cars. "This is serious *art*, Pal. Gaming is . . . Well, it's not art."

Paloma narrowed her eyes at Tara. "You didn't think so when you came over and hogged my console to play Karaoke Kween for, like, seventy-six hours straight."

"Girls, girls," Gemma said, half standing up, looking like a judge as she pressed her palms on the table. "Stop with the childish fight. We've got an important party to plan."

We could always count on Gemma to keep us on track and settle any arguments.

Tara and Paloma grumbled an apology.

"So," Gemma went on, but Tara interrupted.

"Will there be dancing?" she asked, doing one of her signature bhangra dance moves with her arms over her head.

"Um," I said, looking at my other friends, but they just stared back at me, waiting for my answer. Oh yeah, this was *my* party. It was up to *me*. "I *think* there will be dancing. We haven't worked out the details yet."

"Well, there should *definitely* be dancing," Tara said sharply, even though she knew pretty much nothing about bat mitzvahs. But she did know a lot about dancing. "Especially slow dancing, if you know what I mean."

I did. Slow dancing meant boys. My cheeks burned just thinking about it, but before I could think too hard about who I wanted to slow-dance with (Cam Thompson), Paloma changed the subject.

"What about games?" she asked. "We'll get to play some of the carnival and arcade games at the Maize, right?"

"I'm sure. Yeah," I said, making a mental note

to go through the party agenda with my parents, because there were some things like speeches—including one that I would have to make—that I knew they would want to plan. As I thought this, my phone buzzed in my pocket.

I pulled it out to see a pile of texts had come in—RSVPs for the party!

My eyes skimmed down the names (mostly YES responses!) until I saw . . . *gasp* . . . a text from Cameron Thompson!

Dear Yael, this is Cam Thompson, I do not know what a bat mitzvah is but I will find out and let you know if I can attend. Sincerely, Cam Thompson

I twisted my mouth into a frown and looked up at my friends.

"What's wrong?" Tara asked, leaning over my shoulder to read my phone. She snorted. "He's so weird." She read his text out to the other girls while imitating his voice, sounding like a robot.

"I think he's nice," Paloma said. "And he's the best at strategy games in gaming club."

"Hey, did you know that his aunt and uncle own the Maize?" Gemma said.

My heart jumped in my chest. "Really? No, I didn't know that."

Gemma nodded. "Yeah. My mom helped them

out with refurbishing some of the rides." That made sense—Gemma's mom was an electrical engineer.

"Cam works there on the weekends too," Paloma said. "I heard him telling Jin in gaming club that he couldn't go to a hackathon because he had to work."

More information I hadn't known. Huh. As I was thinking about this, I got another text from Cam.

Dear Yael, I have googled what a bat mitzvah is and it sounds cool. Also, my uncle (owner of the Maizo) has informed me that your parents are coming to tour the park this Friday after school. Will you be coming with them? Sincerely, Cam Thompson

WHAT? That was a third, and *even more important*, fact that I didn't know. How had my mother not told me we were going to tour the amusement park?

"What does this mean?" I turned my phone toward my friends so they could read the message. Tara squealed and clapped her hands, while Gemma tilted her head to the side as if she wasn't sure. Paloma just shrugged.

Obviously, no one *really* knew what it meant. Did Cam *want* me to go? Or was he just curious?

"I should go, right?"

Tara said, "Of course! You have to go!" as the other girls nodded enthusiastically.

I took a deep breath and was about to text Cam back with my trembling fingers, when a shadow fell over me.

I looked up to see Eli standing there.

"Hey, Yael. I delivered all the invitations like you asked me to."

I smiled at him. "Thanks. I'm already getting lots of RSVPs."

His eyebrows went up in surprise. "Oh yeah?" Then his voice faltered a little when he added, "I hope a lot of people come to your bat mitzvah."

Ugh. Awkward. "Thanks," I said, trying not to cringe.

At least he moved on quickly. "So hey, are you going to come over on Friday?"

Friday! But what about the tour at the Maize? I looked at my friends for help. Tara was examining her turquoise nails. Gemma waggled her eyebrows, but I didn't know what she was trying to say by that. Paloma shrugged again as she inspected the end of her long braid. They were no help at all.

"Oh, um, yeah," I said, stalling until I figured

this all out. "My mom said something about plans. I'll have to check with her, okay?"

He nodded. "All right." He looked uncertainly at my friends, who all quickly beamed back at him. Like this wasn't already the most awkward conversation ever? "Well, I'd better go."

I said good-bye and guiltily watched him shuffle off.

"What was that about?" Tara asked.

"He's offered to help me with my bat mitzvah stuff."

"I think he likes you," Gemma said, her eyes still on him as he left the cafeteria.

"What?" I demanded.

She turned toward me and nodded. "Yep. I totally think he likes you."

I looked toward the door he'd disappeared through. "Eli?"

"Uh, yeah, the guy who was just here?" Paloma said with an eye roll.

Tara laughed. "For someone as visual as you—who has to, you know, *pay attention*—you can be pretty clueless."

I scrunched up my face. I *had* been paying attention. I had known Eli all my life, and while he was certainly not the Eli of old—not even the Eli of two months ago—he couldn't like *me*. Could he? "No, I just think . . . We've known each other forever."

"He loooooooooves you," Paloma said quietly. When I glared over at her, she smirked.

"Shut up!" I said, looking around to make sure no one had heard.

"He's cute, too," Tara said. "Almost as cute as Cam."

Okay, so if I were to sketch Eli, yes, I might draw thick lines to accentuate his sharper cheekbones. Sure, I would add highlights to his newly bright eyes. I looked at Tara. *Is Eli cute?* It was a surprise to hear it said out loud.

"Eli's less weird than Cam, that's for sure," Tara said. "Maybe you should have a crush on *him*."

Except Cam's weirdness was part of what I liked about him. He said exactly what he meant all the time, and he was really smart and just . . . I don't know, different. But in a good way. Eli was like a still-life painting— nice to look at but nothing unexpected. Cam was like a Salvador Dalí masterpiece—a little strange and always surprising.

Paloma said, "I definitely think Eli's better boyfriend material."

"So," Gemma said, looking at me intently. "What are you going to do?"

I did need to practice my bat mitzvah stuff so I wouldn't totally mess up in front of everyone, and I knew I'd have fun hanging out with Eli, but this was my chance to see Cam. And shouldn't I go tour the Maize since I was having my party there?

Yael goes to Eli's house. Turn to page 46.
Yael goes to the Maize. Turn to page 34.

Splatter

We drove through the giant gates of the amusement park, and I leaned forward as far as my seat belt would allow so I could take in as much as possible. Most of the park was hidden from the street by tall trees, but they couldn't hide the roof of the huge barn, the hills of the roller coaster, and the sky-scraping arc of the Ferris wheel.

As we arrived, I could see other rides: the carousel, the bumper cars, and the tall swings. Faint organ music drifted out toward us, beckoning us to enter the park. A bolt of excitement ran up and down my spine. This place was pure magic.

I wasn't just eager to tour the park, but was also looking forward to seeing Cam. I pulled out my phone and looked at his text for about the five millionth time since it had come in that morning.

Dear Yael, I will meet you and your family at the front gate at 4pm for your tour of the Maize. Sincerely, Cam Thompson

I looked at the little clock on the top of my screen and was relieved to see that, even with some unexpected traffic, we were right on time. I was still impatient when my dad took forever to find just the right parking spot.

Knowing it wouldn't make him move any faster, I pressed my lips together to withhold my plea to hurry up. To distract myself, I turned toward Rivka. "Are you excited to check out the rides?"

"RIDES!" she yelled out, pumping her arms up and down. I smiled, not even sure if she knew what she was so excited about, since she'd never been to an amusement park before.

"We probably won't have time to do more than a few," Mom warned from the front seat.

I glanced over at Rivka, and she was making that deep frown face that meant a tantrum was coming. *Uh-oh.* I grabbed her hand and quickly said, "But we'll for sure be able to try the carousel—you want to ride a horse, don't you, Rivvy? You love horsies!"

Thankfully, that worked, and before even one tear was shed, she began to chant, "Horsie, horsie, Rivvy's gonna ride a horsie!"

Whew! Crisis averted!

Finally Dad found a spot, just in time for us to see Cam walking from inside the park to the ticket booths.

"There's Cam," I said in a weird, high-pitched voice as I exited the car, leaving my parents to deal with getting Rivka set up in her stroller.

It wasn't until I was a few steps away from him that I realized how fast my heart was beating. I was about to meet up with Cam! This definitely qualified as one of Tara's VBDs—a Very Big Deal.

Be chill, I told myself. Ha! Easier said than done. "Hi," I said as I noticed he was wearing a red Maize T-shirt that was tucked into his jeans, making him look taller than normal—way taller than me. His black hair was messy, but I knew from studying him in the cafeteria at school that he ran his hands through it a lot. His amber-brown eyes seemed to be trained over my left shoulder to where my family straggled behind me.

"Welcome to the Maize, Yael," he said. "Thank you for being on time."

"You're welcome." I tried to smile and then turned to see what was taking my family so long. "My parents and sister are coming. Are you going to give us the tour?"

He nodded. "My aunt and uncle are over in the barn—we'll meet up with them there, but I will show you around the park first."

"Great," I said as I heard the rattle of the stroller that signaled my family's arrival. I turned a little and held my arm out. "These are my parents and my little sister, Rivka."

"It's nice to meet you," Cam said politely, giving my parents a wooden smile.

"Where's the HORSIE?!" Rivka blurted out at the top of her lungs, her enthusiasm loud and random, like a Jackson Pollock painting. At least it was a happy outburst and not a tantrum.

Cam shot me an alarmed look.

"We promised her a ride on the carousel," I explained.

"Oh. Okay." Cam smiled at my sister. "Then the carousel should be our first stop," he said, making himself Rivka's new most favoritest person in the world.

. . .

"Ohhhh, this will be perfect!" Mom stretched out her arms as we entered the barn, and I waited for her to spin around like that. She didn't but chattered on nonstop about the reception details with Cam's aunt and uncle while I stood there, stealing glances at Cam.

The plan was that everyone would arrive and then have a few hours to explore the park and go on rides. Then there would be a dinner and all the lame stuff (including the speech I was expected to make—the one I was putting off writing because it was my worst nightmare) and then the dance.

Distracted by Cam, I was only half listening to my mom as she droned on. Cam was currently staring at my sister but seemed to be somewhere else. I got why my friends thought he was weird because he zoned out a lot, but he had a look on his face like he was thinking hard about something. He was super smart, so I supposed he was often lost in thought, and I would have bet that someday he'd solve climate change or would figure out how to harness the energy from bees or something equally clever.

"You okay?" I asked him quietly while my mom began walking around, arranging where the head table would go, where the stage would be, and all the other details I didn't really care about.

Cam shook his head a little and then seemed to focus as he looked at me. "What?"

I cleared my throat. "You looked like you were thinking about something, so I just wanted to make sure everything was okay."

He blinked and then said, "Your sister has a booger."

Wait. What? Did he just say what I thought he said? "Huh?" I said, turning to look, and sure enough, there was a giant crusty right on the end of Rivka's nose. So gross.

"Mom!" I said, interrupting.

"Just a minute, Yael."

"Mom! Rivka has a . . . something." I pointed at my sister and then at my nose.

"So, deal with it," she said in a tone that I knew meant she was annoyed with me for interrupting her. Like it was *my* fault my baby sister had snot problems?

But when I turned to get a tissue from Mom's

bag slung over the back of the stroller, I saw Cam wiping Rivka's face with a napkin.

"You don't have to do that!" I shrieked because my crush had just cleaned my sister's snot.

"I have a little brother who gets boogers all the time," he explained with a shrug.

He finished what he was doing and then looked past me toward my parents and his aunt and uncle. "Fourteen guest tables," he said out of nowhere. "Assuming eight at a table. But we usually estimate ten no-shows, so you could then have nine tables of ten plus one table of twelve."

What?

"Thanks, Cam," his uncle said.

"What was that?" I asked Cam as he tossed the snotty napkin into a garbage can.

"Your mother was asking how many tables you'd need for your party, based on the one hundred and twelve people who are invited."

Oh yeah. Cam was a math whiz.

"Thank you, Cam," my mother said as she and my dad drifted over.

"So this bat mitzvah thing," Cam said quietly. "I did some research, but I don't really understand what it means. It says you'll be an adult, but you can't drive or vote, so . . ." He shrugged and looked at me.

"It means Yael will become a *woman*," my mother said. Then she gave me a knowing smile and opened her mouth, and I suddenly had VERY SERIOUS CONCERNS that she was going to elaborate on the details of *being a woman*. Like, biological details.

"MOTHER!" I interrupted. "A bat mitzvah is when you're called to the Torah in synagogue, and it just means you're now responsible for your actions. It's not about my body or anything like that."

OMG! What had just fallen out of my mouth?

"Your body?" my dad said as he looked from me to my mother and back, making it a thousand times worse. "Who said anything about your body? Wait, you didn't get your—"

Not happening, not happening, NOT HAPPENING!

"NO!" I said, focusing totally on Cam because if I allowed myself to look at my parents, I was going to die of embarrassment. I was already halfway in the grave as it was. "It's just about being a responsible human and a member of the Jewish community in an official way. It's . . . not like . . . It's just about acting more grown-up!"

I wanted to run away but realized that would leave my parents to say more embarrassing things to Cam. It would also be the Opposite of Grown-Up.

In a desperate attempt to end the conversation, I pulled out my phone and noticed that Tara had texted me, asking how it was going.

Ugh, where to start? I didn't have time to respond.

"That sounds cool," Cam said, either clueless about my complete and utter humiliation, or maybe he was the best actor ever.

"I have never been to a synagogue," he said. "But it seems like it would be really interesting. I like learning about different customs and languages."

I was putting my phone away and was about to say that he'd get to learn about Jewish culture at my bat mitzvah, but I didn't get the chance.

"Oh! You should come!" my mother blurted out. "To synagogue, I mean. Next Saturday. Tomorrow! There won't be a bar or bat mitzvah for you to see, but I think you would enjoy a Shabbat service. Especially if you enjoy learning about cultures— you'll love learning about Judaism!"

It was a fitting thing we were at an amusement

park, because my life suddenly felt like a circus. A very *bad* circus. "Mom!" I barked, but it didn't matter, because my sister chose then to go completely nuclear, shrieking something about horsie and candy and whoknowswhatelse—I couldn't focus; my brain had screeched to a halt because of the ridiculousness that was my life.

I darted a look at Cam, who looked like he was having his own internal meltdown.

As Rivka continued to freak out, I grabbed Cam's arm and tugged him toward the door of the barn.

Once we were outside and Rivka's tantrum wasn't quite as eardrum shattering, I realized with horror that I still had a grip on Cam's arm, so I quickly let it go.

"I'm so sorry," I blurted. "About all of that. I . . . ugh, my family."

"I . . . it's . . ." He took a deep breath and shook his head. "I don't like loud noises like that. It's overwhelming sometimes."

Boy could I relate. I nodded and allowed myself a moment to take a few calming breaths as he seemed to do the same. "Anyway," I said, relieved that he seemed to be feeling better now that we were away from Rivka and my parents.

"You don't have to come to shul—synagogue. It's probably not as fun as my mom was making it out to be."

He gave me a funny look like he wasn't sure if I was joking but then said, "Well, it does sound interesting, and I like learning about different things, so I would like to go. But if you don't want me to, that's okay."

I stared at him for a long moment because was he—Cam Thompson, the cute and smart boy who worked at the Maize and who could do crazy math in his head—asking me if he could come to synagogue *with me*?

As he looked at me earnestly, no hint of a joking smile on his face, I realized that yes, he was.

Maybe he was just really interested in learning about Jewish customs like he'd said. As I stared at him, trying to figure it out, his face went a little blotchy.

Having him at shul might be kind of cool, but at the same time, he'd have to deal with my nosy mother and my unpredictable sister. If he *did* like me, would he stop liking me after having to endure more of Rivka's tantrums? Also, did he *really* want to go to synagogue, especially when a lot of the service was in Hebrew? He probably had no idea what he was in for and might just hate it. If that happened, would he be mad at me for encouraging him to go?

———————————

Yael brings Cam. Turn to page 59.
Yael goes without Cam. Turn to page 70.

59
70

Changing the Palette

"Thanks so much for helping me, Eli," I said as he poured green juice into a blender.

We were in his kitchen on Friday after school. I'd arrived with my folder containing my printed Torah portion and was greeted by a whiff of licorice as soon as he opened the door. I'd followed him to the kitchen.

"Happy to help," he said as he lifted the blender lid and scooped out a glop. He sniffed it, frowned, and added a scoop of powder from an unmarked canister—I could smell the tang of ginger. Over his shoulder he said, "Of course you'll do great, but, like the rabbi says, you can never have too much practice.

"Especially when you're really nervous." He added some ice cubes to the blender and let it run for a few seconds more; the loud clatter and grinding halted the conversation. He fetched two mugs and placed them on the counter.

When he turned off the blender, he said, "I was nervous too. But once you get up there, it's not so bad." He divided the concoction between the mugs. "Also, this will help. It's my grandfather's special 'giving a speech' elixir. It's good for your throat, and it's calming, too. And don't worry—it looks gross, but it's really good."

I gave the green drink a sniff, doubting that anything could help with my crazy nerves. I was going to ask him what was in it, but maybe it was better not to know—whatever it was, I trusted him not to poison me. Anyway, I had other problems to focus on.

"But, Eli, I'm not just *kind of* nervous. I'm really, *really* nervous. I think . . . I don't know . . . I think public speaking is my biggest fear. I can't think of anything I'm more afraid of. Except maybe Rivka's tantrums."

He nodded knowingly as we left the kitchen. "No one likes public speaking."

"Not true," I said, following him into the living room. "Tara loves performing. She said if she were Jewish, she'd have a Bollywood bat mitzvah."

Eli laughed. "That would be so cool. Her family would make babka laddus, coconut hamantaschen, naan bagels . . . yummm."

I dropped onto the couch and smiled at the thought of Mr. and Mrs. Singh making Jewish-Indian fusion food at their sweet shop.

"Okay," he said, his voice suddenly serious. "We should start. Do you want to sing your whole portion first? Then we can break it down and work on any parts that are giving you trouble?"

I had just lifted the mug to try a sip and nearly spilled it. "What? You want me to sing it for you?" I put the cup down and looked around. "Here? Now? The whole thing?"

He nodded toward my mug. "Have some of that for your throat first, but yeah." He frowned at me. "No one's around, so Stevie and Adam won't bother us. What did you *think* we were going to do?"

"I don't know," I said, wanting to hide behind a couch cushion, because, seriously, what *had* I thought we were going to do? "You said you'd help me. . . ."

"Yeaaaaaaah . . . ," he said, drawing out the word as he looked at me with widened eyes. "But I can't help you unless I hear you, right?"

"I guess." I felt so stupid as I looked down at the folder, reluctant to open it. Maybe I should have gotten Tara to help me—she knew a lot about performing and rehearsing. Although she didn't know anything about Hebrew, so no, that wouldn't have been very helpful.

Eli came around the table and sat down next to me.

I took a deep breath, filling my lungs up with as much air as I could, attempting the calm-breathing exercise the rabbi had taught us in bar and bat mitzvah class. Then I admitted: "I'm scared."

"I know. It *is* scary. But remember, you only have to do it once." He smirked and added, "*And* you'll get presents no matter how much you mess up."

I snorted at him and rolled my eyes. "It's not all about the presents, Eli."

"I know," he grinned. "But it's still true. No one is there to rate your performance."

I mostly believed him. But even if no one was there to judge me, *I* would be judging my performance and didn't want to embarrass myself. "Also, being a grown-up means that even though you're scared, you do it anyway."

With a sigh I said, "I guess. It just . . . It feels weird doing it in front of you." I wrinkled my nose at him.

He smiled and shrugged. "Yeah, but you're going to have to do it in front of everyone at shul, right? So . . ."

I smacked his arm. "UGH! Don't remind me, Eli!"

He laughed and said, "All the more reason to get started—the more you practice, the better you'll get and the more confident you'll feel about it. Trust me."

"Fine," I said, picking up my folder and taking out photocopied pages. I took another breath and looked at him, giving what I hoped was a confident nod. "Okay. Let's do this."

An hour later—after I'd gone through my Torah portion approximately seventy million times and Eli had given me some feedback and tips—I got a text from my mother to say they were back from the Maize and to come home. I thanked Eli for his help and got ready to leave, looking forward to my mom's special Shabbat roast beef dinner.

But as I left Eli's house, I stopped dead on the front porch; there was a giant van in our driveway. Not just a regular family van like ours, but a business van, painted with balloons and lights and with fancy lettering that said MC MIC ENTERTAINMENT AND EVENTS.

I groaned. *Mother!*

I was about to go back into Eli's house and ask him if I could stay for dinner, when I got another text from my mother. Where are you? Come home now, please!

Great.

I took another one of those calming breaths and went into the house, hanging back and listening, but it was no use—my mother was already *on*, using her loud and braggy, proud-parent voice. The one that guaranteed I was going to be embarrassed.

"And here she is at nine months in the bath—isn't she the cutest? Look at those chubby rolls on her legs!"

Oh. My. Rubber duck. Was she seriously show-ing strangers videos of me as a baby? NAKED IN THE TUB?!

This was not happening.

This was totally happening.

"There you are, Yael!" my mother hollered as I tried (unsuccessfully) to sneak back out the door. "Come in here. I'd like you to meet some people."

I pasted a smile on my face and went into the living room, where my mother had paused the video.

"Heh-heh," she said, her gaze lingering on the TV—our giant big-screen TV, currently display-ing me nearly life-size and naked in the tub—before turning to the two people beside her. "This is Micah and his son, Gabriel. They organize and run parties and will make sure your bat will be the best one ever."

"Best one evah!" my sister repeated, making me glance over at where she was playing with her favorite doll on the floor. She seemed content for now and not about to have one of her legendary tantrums.

Good thing. Because I was about to have one.

"Nice to meet you, Yael," Micah said as he

stood up from the couch and stuck out his hand.

I shook it and gave him what I hoped was a polite smile. "Nice to meet you as well."

"This is my son, Gabriel," he said, gesturing to a teenager beside him. A cute teenager. He was wearing a T-shirt with Hebrew letters that spelled out "Gotham" inside a Batman logo over jeans and a worn pair of black Converse sneakers.

I hoped my hand wasn't sweaty and gross when I put it in his. "Hi. I'm Yael," I said stupidly, because *obviously* I was Yael. Duh.

"Hey," he said, squeezing my hand before he let it go.

And then my eyes flicked back to the frozen TV. Ugh! Heat crept up my face and neck, and I *really* wished I'd stayed at Eli's for dinner.

Micah said, "Your mom was just helping us get together some stuff for the multimedia presentation."

"WHAT?" I demanded, whirling on my mother. "You can't show *that.*"

My mother, certain winner of the Most Clueless Human in the World Award, actually said, "Why not? It's adorable!"

I glanced over at my dad, and he shrugged.

"Maybe I'm biased," he said. "But I think it's adorable too."

"NO!" I yelled then, channeling my inner two-year-old. "NONONONONO! THERE IS NO WAY YOU ARE PLAYING THAT AT MY BAT MITZVAH!"

"Now listen, young lady," my mother said sharply, her hands coming to her hips in her "angry mom" stance.

But I didn't let her finish. I turned and ran.

I fled through the nearest exit I could find—the door leading to the basement. I slammed the door behind me and stomped down the stairs.

When I got to the bottom, I realized I should have taken the extra steps to go up to my room, because now I was trapped in the basement with the shelves of homemade pickles and bookcases filled with photo albums and junk from when I was a baby.

I suddenly *felt* like a baby with the way I'd acted just now, especially in front of Micah and Gabriel. I was so mortified I was vibrating.

As I stood there, trying to figure out how to escape, the door creaked. In about three seconds I would either learn how to disappear or have to deal with a parent.

Wrong on both counts. A pair of Converse sneakers started down the stairs. Which meant I had to deal with the appearance of a cute guy I'd just met who'd seen video of me naked in a tub and then had watched me have a tantrum.

I had just enough time to wonder if I could hide among the pickles before Gabriel was in front of me. "Did my parents send you?" I asked.

"No," he said, shoving his hands in his pockets. "I offered. Your mom said she was going to come and get more pictures of you for the slideshow."

I shook my head. "I'm not putting baby pictures in a stupid slideshow, so if you came down here to find some, you can just go back upstairs right now."

He looked surprised at my angry outburst (though he couldn't have been any more surprised than I was for having made it) and held up his palms toward me as he shook his head.

"No, no," he said. "That's just what I told them. I came down here to tell you that you're right and you should stick to your convictions. I've been doing these parties with my dad since before my own bar mitzvah two years ago, and the ones where parents go crazy with this kind of thing turn into the end of the kid's social life."

"That is *exactly* what I am afraid of," I said, crossing my arms. "How can they be so oblivious?"

He shrugged. "I don't know. Parents seem to forget what it's like to be a kid as soon as they have jobs and stuff, but you shouldn't back down. This is *your* party," he said, looking straight into my eyes. "You should get to do what *you* want."

He was right. I needed to stand my ground and tell my parents that this was *my* party, and we were going to do it my way. "Yeah," I said, straightening my spine, feeling stronger and more confident. "Thank you for being on my side."

"Of course. And maybe we can—"

The door opened, and then Micah yelled down the stairs: "GABRIEL?"

Gabriel tilted his head up toward the door and replied, "Be right there!" Then he turned to me and shrugged. "I should go."

Nooooooooo, what were you going to say? Maybe we can . . . WHAT? I wanted to ask, but I just nodded.

"You should come up too," he said. "So you can tell them you're not doing anything you don't want to do."

"I will," I said. "In a minute." Because first I

needed to figure out what I was going to say.

Gabriel went up the stairs, leaving me alone with my thoughts. And my phone.

I pulled it out, thankful that I hadn't had to turn it off for Shabbat yet. I was going to text Tara, when I saw a message from Cam.

Dear Yael, this is Cam Thompson. I hope you are doing well practicing for your bat mitzvah. Your family came to tour the Maize today and when I told your mother that I have never been to synagogue before, she invited me to attend with you tomorrow. See you there, sincerely, Cam Thompson

I couldn't believe it. There was something worse than the Naked Baby Show. If I could've painted a self-portrait right then, I would have made one giant appalled scribble for my face. It would have looked a lot like Picasso's *Weeping Woman*. For good reason.

Why did my mother have to be so—like my mother? But ugh, it didn't even matter. All that mattered was what I did now. Here was my chance to spend time with Cam. But my family— my *mother*, the woman who seemed to thrive on humiliating me—would be there.

Maybe I should just fake sick, hide from the world, and paint my heart out.

Or maybe it was time for a new Yael. One who got to spend time with Cam.

Yael goes with Cam. Turn to page 59.
Yael stays home. Turn to page 78.

59
78

The Blue Period

Cam was standing outside the synagogue when we arrived, wearing a shirt and tie, looking stiff and uncomfortable. I couldn't tell if it was because of the clothes or where he was. Probably both.

My mother noticed him barely a split second after I did and started cooing like a crazed hen. "Ooooohhhh, look at how dapper Cam looks! He's so handsome."

As annoying as it was to agree with my mother . . . I silently agreed with my mother. He *was* handsome. *So* handsome.

"What a nice boy he is," she said. To whom, I

have no idea. *I* sure wasn't answering.

I tried to get to him first, but my mother left Rivka to my father and nearly sprinted up to Cam, looking like one of those awkward speed walkers we'd watched in the Olympic games. Except way crazier.

Sometimes it felt like her life's goal was to humiliate me. But why did she have to be so successful at it?

"Hi, Cam," I said, hoping he caught the apology in my voice.

He smiled at me. "*Shabbat shalom*, Yael, Mrs. Lewis."

Before I could respond to that, my mother grabbed him by the arm. "*Shabbat shalom*, Cam! Someone has been studying!" she gushed, leading him toward the front doors of the synagogue. I trailed behind them, overcome with dread because services sometimes dragged on, and this was clearly going to be a never-ending one!

Once we got inside, Mom led him over to a box so he could pick out a satin *kippah*. He picked a black one and put it on his head, and I was impressed that he was willing to go so far just to learn about my culture; he really wasn't like any other boy at school.

"Hey, Yael and . . . Cam?" I heard from behind me. I turned to see Eli standing there, looking at Cam with a confused expression.

"Oh, hey," I said. "My mom invited Cam." I goggled my eyes a little, and Eli's smirk told me he understood. The two words "my mom" said it all.

"I'm excited to learn about Judaism," Cam said with a smile.

Eli nodded, looking between us, and I felt heat rise in my cheeks as I realized he was probably wondering what the deal was between Cam and me. Heck, *I* was wondering what the deal was.

"Anyway," I said. "We should get in there."

"Sure," Eli said. "Of course. *Shabbat shalom.*"

And then he left to go join his family, allowing me to let out the awkward breath I'd been holding and focus on Cam.

I grabbed an extra siddur for him, glad that, while most of the service would be in Hebrew, he'd be able to follow along because the book contained English translations. I just hoped he wouldn't be too bored.

Once we got inside the sanctuary, we sat in our regular row, but Mom tried to get Cam to sit between us so she could help him understand the service. I quickly took the spot next to her so he wouldn't be stuck with her over-the-top commentary. He was better off sitting between me and Mrs. Feldman, even though she smelled like mothballs.

I handed him the siddur and smiled when he opened it. "Hold on," I said gently, pointing at it. "You've actually opened it to the back. Hebrew is read right to left."

Cam flipped to the front of the prayer book and scanned the first few pages before looking up at me with a wide smile. "The Hebrew letters look cool. Can you read it?"

I shrugged. "Yeah. And my bat mitzvah will be in Hebrew. The Torah part, anyway."

His eyes went wide. "That is really cool, Yael. I'm looking forward to hearing you read in Hebrew."

"*Sing*," I corrected. "I have to sing it."

His eyes went wider. "Even more impressive."

I blushed then and was about to tell him not to be impressed, since my voice wasn't very good and I still needed to do a lot more practicing, but instead looked down at the book in my lap.

"Thanks for letting me come today," he said, sounding like he really meant it.

I smiled back at him, relieved he wasn't weirded out by my family, and by "family" I meant my mother. "The service should start in a few minutes."

He looked around the room at the other congregants. Most were chatting with their neighbors, waiting for the rabbi.

"Is that a Batman *kippah*?" Cam asked a few moments later. "I didn't know you could have a superhero symbol on a *kippah*."

I followed his gaze to a few rows in front of us.

"That's Gabriel Silver," Mom leaned forward and explained to Cam across me, proving that she'd totally been eavesdropping. "His father the man sitting next to him—is Micah. He owns the company that will be running the music and entertainment at Yael's party. On the Sunday, I mean," she added when Cam stared at her blankly. "On the Saturday, here at shul, it will be *all about* Yael's Torah reading." She glanced at me with teary eyes.

I looked away before I got caught rolling my own and snuck another glance at Gabriel. With his blond hair, striking eyes, and perfectly symmetrical features, he was the cutest guy here.

Whoops, I thought, peeking sideways at Cam,

who was looking up at the stained glass windows. Gabriel was *one of* the cutest guys here.

I looked ahead again, just in time to see Gabriel fully turn around to look at me. It was like he'd heard us talking about him. Or maybe he'd heard me thinking about cute boys.

Urk! I panicked and stared hard at my book, but of course my mother waved and raised her voice. "Hi, Gabriel!" Then she nudged me. "Aren't you going to say hello?"

Um, wasn't planning on it. Thanks for that, Mother. Embarrass me more in front of not one, but two cute guys.

Thankfully, just then, the rabbi came out of his secret room in the back and went up to the podium, signaling a hush in the crowd.

I'd never been so excited for a service to start!

It wasn't a coincidence that I'd invited my friends over that night, knowing they'd want all the details about shul with Cam.

They were interested in hearing about him (and Gabriel, when I told them he was there), but mostly they wanted to talk about the upcoming party—even when I tried to tell them that, while I was worried about the party going well, what

I was *really* worried about were the parts that I had to perform: my Torah portion and then my speech at the party.

I knew Tara couldn't really understand because performing was like breathing to her. And Paloma and Gemma were just super excited, wanting to hash out what they were going to wear, what rides we'd go on, and, of course, which guys they might dance with.

If I could be sure everything coming out of my mouth would be the right thing to say, like the witty dialogue Tara would recite in drama club, I wouldn't worry so much. But only when I was painting and in my own head did I come up with perfect things to say—usually way too late. I stopped trying to get them to understand and let them go on and on.

After my friends left and before I headed up to bed, I padded into the kitchen to steal a mandala cookie from my dad's secret stash because I needed cheering up. The Singhs sometimes sent Tara over with a box of the colorful and delicious cookies—Dad's favorites that he squirreled away. I deserved one after the evening I'd had.

As I stood there, chewing and staring out into

the backyard, I saw a faint glow over the fence that separated our yard from the Roths'.

I smiled, knowing it was Eli out on his hammock with his tablet. I shoved the rest of the cookie into my mouth before I snuck out the back door in my bare feet.

It was dark out, especially in our yard, but I could have found the loose plank in the fence with my eyes closed. When we were eight, I had pried out the nails on one of the boards so we could talk and pass toys through the space.

I gave the secret signal that we'd made up: knock, knock, knock-knock-knock, pause, knock-knock.

"Hey, Yael," Eli said softly. Then the glow of his tablet disappeared, and I heard rustling as he came over to the fence.

I moved the loose board out of the way and said, "Hi, Eli," as he waved his hand through the gap that wasn't big enough to squeeze a whole body through.

"What's up?" he asked. "Everything okay?"

"Yeah," I whispered as I glanced up at the house and the light glowing from my parents' bedroom, not wanting them to hear us. "I saw you were out here, so I thought I'd come say hi."

"Something's wrong," he said. "I can tell."

"I'm okay," I said, but a sigh made its way out before I could stop it.

"Yael, we've been friends forever. Come on, it's me."

I sighed again. "I'm just nervous about everything, you know? I don't want it to be . . ." I trailed off when I realized I'd been about to say *a disaster*, which was exactly what his bar mitzvah had been.

"Like mine?" he filled in.

Ugh. He really did know me. "I didn't mean that," I said, cringing, glad he couldn't see my face.

"I know," he said, thankfully not sounding mad. "But it will be great, and you'll have a great turnout. Everyone is looking forward to it."

"Hold on, I need to get comfortable," I told him as I lay down on the grass beside the gap. More rustling told me he'd done the same on his side. "To be honest, I wouldn't mind if barely anyone showed up. I'm so scared I'll mess up the Torah reading or I'll sound like a dying cat up there. Or that I'll screw up my speech at the party. There are a lot of things I can mess up, Eli. I'm not Tara—I wasn't meant to be on the stage. I wish there was a way to have the whole bat mitz-vah without having to perform, you know?"

He was quiet for a minute, and my throat got all tight because I was sure he thought I *was* going to mess up, that it was inevitable, and he was trying to figure out how to tell me nicely.

But then he said, "Yael, you're not going to mess up. You've been practicing and . . ." He cleared his throat before adding, "You're good at everything you do."

I wiped at my suddenly teary eyes. "You're just saying that to make me feel better."

He snorted. "Well, I do want you to feel better, yeah. But I'm saying it because it's true. You're a talented artist, and you're smart and do well in school. You have lots of great friends, and your family loves you. When you're up there at shul or giving your speech, don't forget that every-one watching is rooting for you. Except Rivka, who'll wonder why you're the one getting all the attention."

I laughed.

"Good," he said in a firm tone. "If I've made you laugh, I've done my job. But I'm serious, Yael; you'll do great. You have nothing to worry about."

"Thanks," I said, not feeling much better about

my ability, but suddenly feeling better about the crowd that I'd be performing for. At least I knew I had one fan.

He gave one friendly little knock on the fence. And then I heard rustling.

"I'm going inside—the mosquitoes are coming out."

"Thanks, Eli," I said as I stood up and brushed off my butt before I slid the board back in place.

"Have a good night, Yael."

I smiled all the way back inside and up to my room. Eli always made me feel better.

Yael goes to the Maize. Turn to page 84.

High Contrast

It was the next morning, and we were sitting in shul as we did nearly every Saturday, except this day was different. It didn't *look* different, with the four of us—Mom, Dad, me, and Rivka (who was dozing off)—sitting in our regular seats, in our nice clothes. But it *felt* different because Cam could have been with me, but I'd told him not to come.

Now that I'd had time to think about it, I was regretting my decision. What was I afraid of? He'd seemed genuinely interested in learning about my world, and I could have explained the customs as he sat beside me.

But I'd chickened out, so now there I sat, my mom on my left and Mrs. Feldman on my right, where Cam should have been. I tried to pretend she was him, but Mrs. Feldman smelled like mothballs, and when she sang, her thin voice was out of tune and wavery.

I glanced over to the left to see Eli, who was sitting with his family a few rows in front of us and on the other side of the aisle, looking at me. He winked and then rolled his eyes and stuck out his tongue.

I smiled and made a face back. But my mother must have noticed and whispered my name in warning. The grin on Eli's face meant he was two seconds from laughing, which would have gotten me going, so I turned away.

As I looked around at the crowd, I noticed a couple of new faces: a boy and a man who looked like they were related—probably father and son, if I had to guess. The boy looked to be about sixteen and had bleached-blond hair, and, as I looked closer, I noticed his *kippah* had a Batman emblem on it. Most of the boys in our synagogue just wore the plain black or white ones that they grabbed from a box in the lobby.

That this guy had his own special one was really cool.

As I openly stared, wondering more about him, he looked over at me.

Meep! Embarrassed at being caught, I quickly looked down at the siddur on my lap, pretending to follow along with the rabbi as he sang the prayers. But as I absently flipped pages, I couldn't help but think about the new boy and how cute he was.

After the service we all filtered out into the hallway. Eli came over and asked me about the tour of the Maize and if I'd gotten to try out any of the rides.

Before I had a chance to answer him, my mom appeared.

"Yael," she said. "I'd like to introduce you to Micah Silver—he's going to be the emcee at your bat mitzvah."

Huh? This was the first I'd heard of even having an emcee. Apparently my blank look didn't clue her in to *my* cluelessness, though. "And this is his son, Gabriel, who is going to help out."

As she said it, my eyes were drawn to the guy

with the Batman *kippah*. I cleared my throat and said, "Hi. Nice to meet you," to both him and his father. It wasn't their fault that my parents hadn't told me any of this.

"So, Micah, I was thinking that . . . ," Mom began, apparently done with the introductions as she pulled the man away from us and started speaking to him intently in a low voice.

I turned to Gabriel, when Eli jumped in, reminding me he was there as he stuck his hand out for a shake. "Hey, I'm Eli Roth. Cool *kippah*."

Gabriel gave a short nod and shook Eli's hand. "Thanks."

"So . . . you new in town?" Eli asked.

"Yeah, sort of," Gabriel said with a shrug. "My dad just moved to Knot's Valley, so I visit on weekends and help with his event business."

"Eli! Time to go," Mrs. Roth called out from near the entrance. We waved hello at each other.

Ugh, don't go! I wanted to say, afraid of being left alone with this cute, older guy I didn't know. But Eli had already said good-bye and was weaving through the crowd toward his family.

"So," Gabriel said, once Eli was gone. "Your party's at the Maize, huh? That's cool."

I shrugged, feeling shy.

"Something wrong?"

I looked up at him. His eyes were not quite blue and not quite green—something in between with flecks of brown. "Wasn't my first choice."

He gave me a confused look. "What do you mean?"

"I just wanted to have it at a restaurant with a few friends."

"Really?" His eyes widened, and his brows shot up to the top of his forehead, almost disappearing beneath his blond hair. "I've done a ton of parties with my dad, and I've never known anyone to *not* want a big party. Especially at the Maize."

I shrugged again. "I'm not into big parties. I don't like being the center of attention."

As soon as I said it, I realized I was confessing this to a complete and total stranger. I thought he was going to make fun of me for not wanting a party, but he just tilted his head to the side and said, "Then why are you having one?"

It was such a reasonable question, I could have cried right there.

I glanced over my shoulder and saw that my parents were still busy talking to Gabriel's father, the three of them intently discussing something. "For my parents," I said with a sigh. "Mostly my mom, actually. She wants it to be a big deal. Having it at the Maize was my compromise for having a party at all, but it's still going to be this huge thing where I have to do a speech and everyone will look at me. I mean, it's supposed to be about being called to the Torah, right?"

"Yeah, that's the important part." The way he said it convinced me that this guy, this mysterious stranger with a Batman *kippah*, got it. He got *me* after knowing me for all of two seconds, when my own parents, who'd known me my whole life, didn't.

He leaned in close.

"So why don't you bail?" he whispered.

I glanced at my parents again, but they were still busy. "I can't bail on my own bat mitzvah."

"Not the whole thing," he said as he widened the gap between us. "The parts you don't want to do."

"What do you mean?"

He looked around and then leaned in again, even closer this time. "The speeches and stuff. Just be 'missing' when it's time for them. The Maize is a big place; I'm sure you could get 'lost,' right?"

Wait. Was he telling me to skip out on my speech? I asked him just that, and he shrugged. "Sure. It's *your* day. Why shouldn't you be able to do what *you* want to do?"

It made sense. A lot of sense, especially when I hadn't wanted the party in the first place, except . . .

"Don't worry," he said. "I can help you. I've done a ton of these parties, and I've been to the Maize, so I can show you the best places to hide out."

It sounded so tempting.

"Maybe . . . ," I began, thinking of the possibilities.

"Come on, Yael," he said. "It will be your only bat mitzvah—what are you going to do? Be the girl your parents want you to be who does 'the right thing' all the time, or put Yael first and be the girl who's true to herself, even if it means being a bit of a rebel?" He lifted a mischievous eyebrow and added, "Or maybe *especially* if it means being a rebel."

Well, when he put it like that . . . I'd always been a good girl, doing the right thing all the time, but being a rebel sounded thrilling.

Maybe it was time I looked out for Yael first and did my own thing.

Yael follows the original plan. Turn to page 84.
Yael rebels. Turn to page 106.

84
106

A Messy Collage

"Uuuuuooooooooohhhhhhhhh," I moaned loudly from the bathroom, hoping a parent would hear it through the door. I'd been in there, groaning, for something like twenty minutes.

I listened at the door. Still nothing.

Pressing my face against the seam of the closed door, I tried again. "OOOUUUUUGHHH. MY STOMACH!"

The little show I was putting on (Tara was going to be so impressed) was totally embarrassing but was still *way* less embarrassing than it would have been to sit next to Cam in shul while he was subjected to my family. Not to mention Mrs. Feldman, the old lady who sat beside us who was nosy and always smelled like mothballs.

"Yael?" my father said.

Finally! Sheesh, took long enough!

I let out another loud moan and then weakly called out, "Yeah, Dad. I'll be ready for shul in a min—ooooohhhhhhhhhh."

"You okay in there?"

"I'm . . . ooooohhhhhhhh . . . um . . . yeah, I'm fine. Just give me a minute." I flushed and then tousled my hair and half closed my eyes before I opened the door a bit. "Sorry, Dad, I'm almost ready," I said weakly. "I'll get dressed."

"Yael? What's wrong?" he asked, frowning in concern.

"Just . . . a little upset stoma—uh-oh." I ducked back into the bathroom, slammed the door in his face, and sat on the toilet lid. "Just give me a few minutes. I *really* want to go to shul," I yelled in a strained voice.

"You're not going anywhere. You sound awful."

YES!

"No, Dad," I moaned. "I *want* to go. My bat mitzvah is soon, and I think I should be—uggghhhhh."

"What's going on here?" I heard my mother say. Shoot. She was always the harder sell. I stared at the closed door, wishing I'd locked it, because there was a chance Mom might come in—she was immune to all gross things.

"Yael's not feeling well," Dad answered for me as I moaned my "encore performance," as Tara would say.

"What's wrong?" Mom asked, thankfully staying on her side of the door. Her low tone told me she was asking Dad, so I got closer to the door to listen. "Did she get her . . ." Her voice trailed off even lower. I slapped my hand to my forehead.

This was going from pretend embarrassing to *really* embarrassing in a hot minute.

I yanked the door open. "I have stomach problems, Mom," I said with a pointed look before I slammed the door again, locking it this time.

"Better not be the flu," Dad grumbled. "I can't afford to get sick."

Don't worry, you won't, I wanted to tell him, but wasn't about to blow my story.

I had thought to blame Mom's Shabbat roast, but that was not a good tactic when no one else was sick. Plus, I loved her roast and didn't want to risk her not making it again. "I traded a kid part of my cheese sandwich for the egg salad from his locker yesterday at school," I said. "I'm sure that's it."

"Oh, kid, not a good idea," Dad said.

"Do you need me in there?" Mom asked, jiggling the handle. Thank goodness I'd locked it!

"Mom, I'm not Rivka. I can manage."

"Fine," she huffed. "Will you be okay on your own if we go to shul?"

"Yes," I said. "I'll be okay. I'll make sure to hydrate."

"Good," Mom said. "We'll be back after kiddush. I'll take my cell just in case. Don't forget phone off unless it's an emergency, understood?"

"Yes, Mother," I said, not even needing to fake *that* groan.

"How are you calling me?" Tara asked when she answered her phone a half hour later, which was exactly one minute after I watched our car—containing my family—pull out of the driveway. My bestie knew I wasn't supposed to use my phone on Shabbat, which often seemed like an unfair rule when she and I needed to talk but today felt like an impossible one.

"This qualifies as an emergency," I said, and

proceeded to tell her everything, from how my parents wanted to do the Slideshow of Humiliation, to my mother inviting Cam to synagogue, to the subject of Gabriel. I told her how his smarts had convinced me to stand my ground with my parents to great results: They had finally agreed there would be no Slideshow of Humiliation. (Cue my complete and utter relief.)

I sighed.

"What's wrong?" Tara asked.

"I'm such a chicken."

"Huh?"

"I could be sitting in shul next to Cam Thompson right now, but instead, I faked explosive bowel syndrome, and he's probably stuck sitting next to Rivka."

There was a long pause on the phone. Then: "Uh, Yael?" Tara said, and I could hear the cringe in her voice.

"What?"

"Um, well, I . . . I, uh . . . I hope she didn't, but do you think your mother told him you aren't there because of your explosive bowel syndrome?"

"I NEVER EVEN THOUGHT OF THAT!" I yelled into the phone. "Oh no. I'm so doomed. I may as well upload the Slideshow of Humiliation to the Internet. My social life is OVER."

"Yael," Tara snapped. "Stop feeling sorry for yourself. It will all be fine. You'll see."

I doubted it. But Tara could be a force. Maybe she'd get me out of this mess somehow.

"You do your thing at the shul, of course, but at the party just concentrate on your friends— your *girl* friends. We'll have a great time, right? And no boy pressure."

I smiled for the first time in what felt like days. I loved my friends, and Tara was right that we would have fun. But was I being a chicken by avoiding Gabriel (and Cam)? Did being a grown-up mean getting over my awkwardness— even if it meant forcing it, even if it meant not being *me*?

Yael goes for Gabriel. Turn to page 106.
Yael focuses on her friends. Turn to page 122.

106

122

Triptych

Party day! Finally!

I was so excited!

Mostly.

The day before, I had nailed my Torah reading. All that practice had really paid off.

I had been so nervous when we walked into the synagogue, and it felt so strange to leave my family and friends sitting in our regular row while I had to sit in the front until the Rabbi called me up. My heart was thumping so quickly I could barely concentrate on the service, and I almost missed my cue to stand up to lead the Aliyah, but

Eli started having a coughing fit behind me until I snapped back to reality.

I mustered all the courage of the woman I was about to become, and walked up to the bimah to recite the Aliyah. As I looked out into the crowded synagogue, I saw my family and friends beaming up at me, and I knew that even if I stumbled through the reading, they'd be proud of me no matter what.

After leading the Aliyah, I glanced at my mom, who mouthed the words "I love you" just as I took a deep breath and began my Torah portion. It felt like time stood still as I sang the words, but I tried to channel all of Tara's talent and confidence as I made my way through it. And it worked! I didn't forget any words, and I think my voice only cracked once, so I'll take that as a win. When it was all over, I returned to my seat and looked forward to celebrating with the congregation at the Kiddush brunch in the hall. I had survived and lived to tell the tale!

After that, I had convinced myself that if I could *sing* that whole thing *in Hebrew* and only stumble a little, I could do a speech in English. And it's not like I had to memorize what to say—I'd printed it out, and it was now currently folded up and stuffed into my pocket for later. Easy-peasy. Or so I told myself, determined to be brave *and* responsible.

We arrived at the Maize, and I let myself enjoy the moment. All my friends and relatives were coming to this wonderful place and that guaranteed an amazing time. I felt pretty lucky.

As Dad pulled into a spot (after circling the parking lot *only* twice), I saw Tara, Paloma, and Gemma waiting for me by the ticket booths. They were all smiling so hard; Tara was even bouncing on her toes in anticipation.

Seeing them so excited was contagious, and I barely waited for the car to stop before I unbuckled my seat belt and launched out of the back seat, ignoring my mother yelling my name and something about being run over by my own father.

"YAEL!!!" Tara hollered, pulling me into a crushing hug with one arm as she held the other out with her phone to take a selfie. "You finally arrived!"

"I'm a half hour early!" I laughed as she let me go, only to be grabbed into Paloma's waiting arms. Then I pulled back from Paloma so Gemma could have her turn.

"We've been here for twenty minutes already,"

Gemma said, holding up her phone. "I wanted to capture you arriving."

Leave it to Gemma to think of everything.

"Where to first?" Paloma asked. "Can we go play games?"

While I wanted to say yes, the grown-up thing to do would be to go to the barn first to check the room setup and get ready to greet people.

"Come on, girls," my mom said as she joined us, pushing Rivka in her stroller. "Let's get inside. You can go run off and have fun soon, but first Yael needs to welcome everyone."

I knew it. Time to be a grown-up.

The moment I entered the barn, I stopped, suddenly overwhelmed. I looked around at the twinkling fairy lights, the antique wooden tables decorated with red-and-white gingham tablecloths, and the buckets filled with candy that served as table centerpieces. There were bundles of cornstalks and hay bales arranged around the hall, adding a crisp, earthy smell. It made me immediately think of a Maud Lewis painting—charmingly rustic, the same look I'd been going for with my invitations.

I'd been so silly to ever *not* want this party.

I turned and looked at my mom, taking a deep breath so I wouldn't cry. "Thank you so much," I whispered.

She put her arm around me. "See? I told you you'd love it, Yael."

My mother could be over the top sometimes, but I was suddenly so glad I'd listened to her. My friends were squealing as they flittered around the room, taking a million pictures of themselves and the decorations. Tara made duck lips and draped her arm around a scarecrow as Gemma snapped a picture of her. I shook my head at her but couldn't help grinning at the scene, loving that they were already having a great time even before the party started.

A loud clanging drew my attention to the stage where Gabriel and his dad were setting up the big stage lights and speakers.

Tara danced up beside me. "Who is that?" she muttered, barely moving her lips.

I glanced over at her, and she waggled her eyebrows and darted her eyes toward the stage. "Is that him?"

"Gabriel," I said, trying my best not to blush (and failing). "And that's his dad. He's the emcee for the dance."

"Ahhhh," she said knowingly. "He's really cute."

"Shhhhh!"

"Be cool," Tara said out of the side of her mouth. "He's coming over."

"Seriously?"

I looked at Gabriel.

"Hey, Yael. Love your shirt."

I glanced down at my silver YAEL'S BAT T-shirt, on which I'd painted a blue bespectacled robot.

My mom had actually ordered me a shirt online that said BAT MITZVAH GIRL on it where the "girl" was crossed out and the word "woman" was written on top, but I told her that I didn't care *how* adorable she thought it was, I was not going to wear it. Nope. Not ever.

She thought I was joking, but when I showed up at the breakfast table the next day with this masterpiece, she gave in and said she'd return the other one. She could save it for Rivka if she wanted; I didn't care, as long as *I* didn't have to wear it.

I looked down at my shirt with pride. Taking more ownership of my life felt pretty good.

When I looked back up at Gabriel and thanked him, he was smiling at me in a way that made my knees feel like noodles. I turned and introduced him to my friends, hoping that taking the focus off me would help with my sudden jitters.

He nodded politely at everyone. "So I have to stick around here to work while you all get to go on rides, but maybe later I'll get to dance with the bat mitzvah girl?"

"That's you," Tara whispered, but not very quietly. "He wants to dance *with you*."

I almost died because: *TARA! He's standing RIGHT THERE!*

She suddenly jumped, hissing something, which I was pretty sure meant Paloma had just kicked her in the shin to get her to shut up. *Thank you, Paloma!*

I nodded up at Gabriel.

"Hi, Yael!" Micah called from up on the stage before he nodded at his son. "Can you come back up here, Gabe? I need you to load this T-shirt cannon."

"Back to work," Gabriel said with a shrug before he turned and jogged away.

"He is seriously cute," Gemma said. "Tara, cover me so I can get some pictures."

The whole lot of them were trying to kill me with embarrassment.

"Speaking of cute," Paloma said, looking over my shoulder as she nodded toward the door. "Cam just arrived."

I turned to look at my crush but almost bashed into someone—Eli.

"Oh, hey!" I said, taking a step back. "I'm so glad you're here."

"I . . . uh . . . I wouldn't have missed it," he said, his eyes darting around. "Here's your present," he said, shoving a gift bag toward me.

"Oh!" I said, taking the bag automatically. "Thanks!"

"It's a star."

"What?" I asked, looking down into the bag, stupidly expecting it to be glowing. It wasn't. I looked back at Eli, who *was* glowing . . . bright red.

"Not a real one, of course." He laughed nervously. "But, uh, I registered one in your name."

"Whoa," Tara said, beating me to it as she looked at me with widened eyes. "That's so cool."

"Thanks, Eli," I said. "That's really nice." He'd obviously given his gift some thought.

"You're—"

Just then a blast of party music came out of the giant speakers, cutting Eli off and getting everyone's attention. A cheer erupted, and I looked around, surprised at the crowd. While I had been mooning over Gabriel, the barn had filled up with people.

The music faded out, and Gabriel's dad came to the microphone. "Good afternoon, everyone!" he said into the mic in his booming emcee voice. Everyone turned to look toward the stage. "Welcome to Yael Lewis's EPIC BAT MITZVAH PAAARRRTAAAAAAY!"

Cheers and screams went up from the crowd. Paloma let out one of her really loud wolf whistles. Once that died down a little, he continued. "I'm your host, MC Mic, and I'm here to make sure everyone has a good time." He paused for more cheers. "There will be prizes for the best dances, the craziest dances, the loudest cheers, and the best singing, along with a few other surprises I have up my sleeves. But before we get the dance party started, you all have some time out in the Maize to enjoy yourselves. On your way out, grab yourself one of the wristbands that will give you access to all the rides.

"Just make sure you're back by six—we'll make an announcement on the park's PA system at five forty-five, and the first table to get all its people back and seated wins a prize! Until then, have a great afternoon!"

More cheers erupted, and I looked around at my family and friends. Everyone was there to have a good time, and it was all because of me and my bat mitzvah. I suddenly felt pretty darn good about my life choices. Even the ones that hadn't really felt like choices.

"Come on," Tara said, grabbing my arm and pulling me toward where Gabriel was standing by the door, giving out wristbands. "I want to get on the bumper cars."

"No, to the games!" Paloma said, holding up a strip of tickets. "I'm all ready to kick butt!"

"It's Yael's bat mitzvah," Gemma said. "*She* should get to decide. Although I hope she chooses the roller coaster," she added with a wink.

I didn't care, as long as I was with my friends. They pulled me toward the exit, but I suddenly remembered Eli, feeling bad that I'd abandoned him. I looked around and saw him across the barn, squatting down to chat to Rivka while my parents were talking animatedly with the caterer.

Before I could do anything, Tara ripped his present from my hands and tossed it onto the gift table. "Come on, bat mitzvah girl!" she exclaimed, and tugged me toward the exit.

We started with the teacups, which was crazy fun, and we all shrieked with laughter the whole time. We kept trying to squash one another into the wall of the giant cup as it whirled around and around.

When the ride was over and we climbed out, I felt like my brain had been scrambled. I stuck my hand in my pocket and was relieved that, after all the knocking around on the ride, the folded-up page of my speech was still there.

"Want to go again?" Gemma asked.

"Not even a little," I said, heading toward the exit before my other friends got other ideas.

"Hey, Yael," Cam said, appearing out of nowhere.

I smiled at him. "Cam! Were you on the teacups?"

He shook his head. "No. They make me ill.

I like the Ferris wheel best. But also the roller coaster."

"Oh, that's perfect!" Gemma exclaimed from behind us. "Because the roller coaster is *exactly* where we're going next! You'll come with us, right, Cam?"

I fought the urge to glare at Gemma, who was being SO OBVIOUS.

"I have enough time for one ride," Cam said with a nod.

"I wish you didn't have to work," I said wistfully.

"My uncle's a bit short-handed today," Cam said. "I'm just helping out a little. I'll be done before dinner starts."

"Oh, that's good." Cute *and* conscientious!

He looked over at me as we walked. "Are you having fun at your party so far, Yael?"

"Very much," I said. "Though, I'm a little nervous about my speech later."

"How come?"

I shrugged. "I don't like public speaking, and I'm worried it's stupid."

"Why?" he asked.

I pulled the paper out of my pocket and unfolded it, starting to think I hadn't worked on it enough. I'd spent so much time working on my Torah portion that I'd sort of just thrown the speech together last minute. "I don't know—I just . . . I don't know."

"May I read it?" he asked, holding his hand out.

I was about to say no but figured he was going to hear it later anyway, so I handed it to him.

His eyes scanned the page as I held my breath. Then, when I thought I might suffocate, he finally looked up and handed the paper back to me. "It's not stupid."

I exhaled. "Oh."

"I don't mean that I didn't like it," he clarified. "Just that you said you were worried it was stupid. It's not. It's clever, and I liked it very much."

"Oh!" I said again, but this time my heart lifted. "Thanks, Cam."

He nodded.

And that's when I ran out of things to say.

Apparently, so had he.

This wasn't really surprising. Cam was the sort of guy who spoke when he had something important to say. He definitely wasn't a babbler, which I appreciated, especially since my friends were big talkers. Like my best one, who was currently behind me, telling anyone within hearing distance that funnel cake was okay but nowhere near as good as the treats from her parents' sweet shop.

As our silence stretched on, I couldn't think of anything else, and it started to get awkward.

Talk to him! I silently pleaded with myself. *Say something!*

Talk to me! I silently pleaded with him.

But he wasn't psychic or couldn't think of anything to say either.

We finally arrived at the roller coaster, which had a line longer than the synagogue buffet at last year's Hanukkah party. Luckily, my friends filled the silence with their excited chatter about the ride.

When we got to the front of the line, Gemma and Paloma paired up as expected. But then Tara linked arms with Katy de la Cruz, a girl from her drama club. Katy looked confused, which made two of us. Then Tara leaned in really close and said, right into my ear, "Sit with Cam."

Nausea and terror could not be any less romantic, but it was too late to back out now. The coaster had pulled in, and the last riders were already getting out of the cars. I scanned their faces, and, thankfully, none of them looked *too* traumatized.

I took a breath and followed Cam, trying to make myself as small as possible as I climbed in beside him. Of course our shoulders and legs still touched as we adjusted ourselves in the narrow car. The lady on the loudspeaker welcomed us to the ride and warned us to keep our hands inside the cars and to stay seated at all times. Cam pulled the safety bar down and double- and then triple-checked it, which I appreciated. Very much.

"Are you afraid?" he asked.

I stared straight ahead—WHY were we at the very front, where I would see *everything*?—and nodded. "I've never been on a roller coaster like this one before." Or *any* roller coaster, but he didn't need to know that.

He said, "Don't be alarmed when it feels like it's going to break apart."

I looked him full in the face. "*What?*"

"That's just part of the ride—the wooden beams are very structurally sound, but one of the things avid roller-coaster enthusiasts enjoy about wooden rides is that they shake a lot. Especially as they age. This one's pretty old."

"Are you trying to make me feel better?" I squeaked.

He looked at me and tilted his head in confusion. "Yes. That's why I said 'don't be alarmed.'"

"Oh, okay," I said, now *extremely* alarmed.

He stared at me for a moment and then said, "Should we hold hands?"

I blinked at him. If I were to paint a self-portrait right then, it would be of just two giant crazed eyeballs.

One of the things I really liked about Cam was that he always meant what he said, but we'd never been in this kind of situation before. Was he just trying to be reassuring, or did he *want* to hold my hand? He hadn't seemed to mind when Tara had made us sit together, but it's not like he had any friends with him that he'd rather sit with.

As all this went through my head, he was staring at me, waiting for my answer.

It came three-tenths of a second later when the car lurched toward the giant hill of track that ran over very shabby-looking wood beams. I grabbed his hand.

I'm okay. I'm okay. I'm okay.

"Sorry if my hand's all sweaty," I said as we

started up the hill.

"Sweating is a normal bodily function that serves to aid in thermoregulation or, probably in this case, can be caused by stress," Cam said.

"Right," I said as we approached the crest of the hill. "Okay, yeah, stress. Definitely stress."

Cam squeezed my hand a little, so I gave him the best smile I could. It probably looked like a death grimace.

We got to the top of the hill, and the coaster seemed to just hang there for an eternity. I thought it was broken and was about to say something to Cam, but then he squeezed my hand hard. I had half a second to wonder what that meant before our car jerked forward and made a loud *ka-chunk*.

And then it let go.

After Cam left to return to work, I went one more time on the roller coaster with my friends so I could experience it with my eyes open and without screaming like I was being murdered. Then after a ride on the carousel and several failed attempts to win something on the midway, we heard the announcement from MC Mic to return to the barn.

I was ready for dinner. We'd burned up a ton of adrenaline and needed fuel.

As the four of us walked back to the barn, I listened to my friends talk—about the rides, the games, and how they wished *they* could have bat mitzvahs. I felt proud that I'd found a way to make my parents, my friends, and even me happy. Maybe solving problems *was* easier now that I was officially a grown-up.

"Yael?" Gemma said, leaning into my shoulder. "Did you hear anything we just said?"

I looked from her to my other friends, realizing I hadn't. "Oh, no, sorry."

Tara rolled her eyes. "I asked you who you were going to have your first slow dance with."

I had been so busy worrying about everything else that I hadn't even thought about it. "Oh, I . . ."

"It's really important," she said. "The person you dance with will be your boyfriend."

Paloma let out a loud *tsk* and then turned to me and said, "That's not true. You can dance with anyone, and that doesn't mean he's your boyfriend."

"Although," Gemma said, "the first guy you dance with probably means you like him more than the others."

"Still important," Tara said, her voice a little pouty.

Paloma went "Pffft," but Gemma looked at me intently. "So? Who do you want to dance with, Yael? Gabriel? Cam?"

I thought about Gabriel and how he'd said he wanted to dance with me. Cam had always been my crush, but Gabriel had *specifically* said he *wanted* to dance *with me*.

But Cam had held my hand on the roller coaster. He was cute *and* nice.

"Don't forget Eli," Paloma said, interrupting my thoughts. "He's totally into you too."

"What?"

"Oh please," Tara said. "Did you not see how he was when he gave you that star? He was all nervous and adorable."

I had noticed, but it still felt weird to think of Eli liking me that way. I looked at Gemma and Paloma, who were nodding along. Did they all think it?

"So, who do you want to dance with?"

"I don't know!" I thought back to when I'd been talking to Gabriel. How mature and tall and *confident* he was. It was thrilling to be with someone so . . . grown-up. "I . . . I think Gabriel's pretty cool, but . . . I'm just not sure. Maybe I'll figure it out when we get back inside."

"Good plan," Gemma said. "As long as you figure out it should be Cam."

"Wrong. Gabriel, obvs," Tara said.

I looked at Paloma, who shrugged. "I think Eli's a good match for you."

I shook my head. "You guys are no help AT ALL!" They all laughed, although I was only half joking.

Then, as we came around the corner of the big corn maze, I noticed Gabriel standing there, leaning against one of the wooden signposts. His back was to us, and it only took a second to realize that he was holding his cell phone to his ear.

"Ooooh, there's your new boyfriend," Tara said. "Go talk to him," she added, putting her hand on my back and giving me a little shove toward him.

"Shhh," I whispered at her, hoping he would hurry up and end his call so he could turn around and remember that he wanted to dance with me.

I stood there, patiently waiting for him to

finish on the phone, when he shifted his weight from one foot to the other. "Yeah, for sure, Jenny," he said as he nodded. "I should be done working by nine. Not much later—it's one of those kiddie parties where I have to pretend like I want to hang out with all the tweens. . . . Ha-ha—it's not so bad. They treat me like I'm a rock star. . . . Hey, why don't you meet me here, and we can get lost in the corn maze?"

Kiddie parties?

Paloma angrily grabbed my arm and pulled me away. "What a jerk!"

At the same time, Gemma huffed, "Not worth your time. Come on, Yael." She grabbed my other hand and, together with Paloma, tugged me toward the barn. "Forget about him, and let's have fun."

"Yeah!" Tara added, grimacing at Gabriel, even though he still had his back turned.

While I was glad for my friends, I still couldn't believe what he'd said. I'd thought he was being nice, but obviously he was just pretending. Would I ever understand guys? I suddenly didn't feel quite as grown-up anymore.

Done with Gabriel and his jerky games, I let my friends lead me into the barn. I was hurt, but at least my choice of who to dance with first was now narrowed down to two: Eli, my oldest friend, or Cam, my longtime crush.

Yael chooses Eli. Turn to page 147.
Yael chooses Cam. Turn to page 137.

Self-Portrait

I didn't even want to go. Of course, it was my party and all my friends would be there, but after yesterday's disaster, when I'd messed up my Torah reading, I was afraid of what more the universe had in store for me when it came to all things bat mitzvah.

But no matter how much I wanted to, there was no bailing on my giant party. Not only would my parents be upset, but my friends would be too.

This was *supposed* to be the party of the year.

It was going to be the joke of the century.

At least we got to the Maize early so no one was there yet. Mom and Dad got Rivka into her stroller without incident. I would've normally enjoyed the peace, but I could've used the distraction of a tantrum. What did *that* say about my current state of mind?

We made our way into the old barn that had been set up for the party in a really pretty rustic farm theme. There were hay bales and some giant stalks of corn tied to the beams. Each of the tables had a centerpiece made of a miniature scarecrow on a stick, planted in a clay pot, and even in my current bad mood, I had to admit they looked good. Score one for Mom.

Metal clangs and shouts brought my attention up to the stage, and we looked over to see Micah and Gabriel working along with a few other guys. They were setting up big lights and speakers. It looked like they were preparing for a concert. I'd seen this sort of thing at other bar and bat mitzvahs and thought it was pretty cool, but at mine it just felt . . . intimidating.

I didn't want this. I didn't want this, I thought, turning away from the stage, fighting tears.

"It all looks great," my oblivious mother said, her eyes wide with awe as she took in the room.

"The kids are going to have such a great time."

Not all *of them,* I didn't say as I started toward the bathrooms, wanting to be alone.

I was almost there when I heard, "I like your shirt."

I turned to see Cam smiling at me.

Looking down, I was reminded that my mother had made me wear the lame shirt she'd ordered for me online that said BAT MITZVAH GIRL on it, where the "girl" was crossed out and "woman" was scribbled on top. Somehow, *she* didn't think that was embarrassing. Like it wasn't bad enough that *she* was wearing a shirt that said I CAN'T KEEP CALM. I'M THE BAT MITZVAH MOM!

Oy vey!

"Thanks," I muttered at Cam. Things had been a bit weird since my mother had invited him to shul that Saturday morning and I'd totally avoided the situation. Though I was glad to see him here at my party. And that he was smiling at me meant that maybe he wasn't feeling awkward, and it was all in my head. It wouldn't be the first time.

"I saw the guy from the party company loading some shirts into a special cannon," he said.

"They're going to shoot them out later during the dance."

At least *those* shirts, emblazoned with the phrase I SURVIVED YAEL LEWIS'S BAT MITZVAH AT THE MAIZE! were cool. Not sure why I couldn't wear one of those to my own bat mitzvah party, but whatever.

I glanced over my shoulder toward the stage, but Gabriel wasn't there. Maybe he was unloading stuff from their van. I turned my head back to Cam, who was waiting for me to speak. "Yeah, they're shooting those out, and they're doing a bunch of dance contests and other things," I said, trying to smile even though I felt like a Picasso painting—one from his Blue Period.

"Everything okay?" he asked, bending down to look into my eyes. Which made me feel worse.

"Fine, thanks," I said, suddenly breathless. "I need to go use the ladies' room. Excuse me."

Before he could stop me, I headed over toward the bathroom, pulling my phone out to see all the texts that were coming in from my friends. There was a group message from Paloma, Tara, and Gemma, saying they'd arrived and were heading toward the rides, asking me when I was going to join them. For the first time that day, I felt relief and maybe even a tiny bit happy. I told them to wait for me by the carousel, and I'd meet them there as soon as I could.

A few hours with my friends on rides and playing games was exactly what I needed. We had so much fun and laughed so much that I was able to forget how I'd messed up at shul the day before. I even almost forgot about my upcoming speech.

Until we were about to head into the corn maze and I looked at my phone to check the time. We only had about twenty minutes until the reception was supposed to start, and my parents would expect me back at the barn.

"I should head back," I said to my friends. "The party's going to start soon."

"You have time," Tara said. "Let's just go in here and race to the middle. Then we'll all go back. It'll be fun!"

Paloma and Gemma agreed, looking excited.

"Okay," I said, not wanting to go back just yet. "First one to the middle gets . . ."

Before I could think of the perfect prize, Tara blurted, "To pick the first song to dance to."

"Oh, it's on!" Paloma said, because we'd already had a huge discussion about which was the best first dance to start the party. Tara wanted a song by Chumz (her favorite boy band), of course, Paloma thought the "Chicken Dance" would be funny, while Gemma picked something old-school that I'd never heard of. And I, well, I had no idea what I'd choose. All I could think of was the speech I was going to have to make. Very soon.

As my friends scattered into the maze, I was left standing at the entrance, paralyzed by indecision.

Suddenly there was a body beside me.

"Hey, Yael," Gabriel said.

I looked over at him and smiled. He'd changed into one of my bat mitzvah shirts. "Hi."

"It's almost time," he said with a crooked grin.

"I know," I said, not needing him to say what it was almost time for. I waved my hand toward the entrance. "My friends are in the maze."

He pointed with his chin. "So how come you're not?"

Because I couldn't decide on a song? Because I'm too nervous? Because you're *here?* I didn't say any of those things and just shrugged.

"Come on," he said, grabbing my hand and tugging me into the maze with him.

All thoughts about my speech flew out of my head. He was holding my hand!

"Where are we going?" I asked. *Duh. Into the maze.* My brain was an abstract painting, all splotches and swirls shaped like question marks.

"Trust me," he said.

I nodded, excited to be with him, thankful he seemed to know where he was going. We rushed past the tall cornstalks making shushing noises in the breeze, the strategically placed (fake) crows and scarecrows looking out at us. Then I heard some squeals and laughing close by—my friends had obviously run into each other. I wanted to find them to show them who I was with, but while I looked toward where the sound was coming from, the corn was too dense to see through. I was on my own with Gabriel.

He turned back and winked at me. "Almost there."

I just nodded and smiled back, hoping he knew his way, because I was already completely lost. Whatever. I was more concerned about figuring out how to take a selfie of us without it being weird.

Finally, we turned a corner and found ourselves in the center of the maze. It was a clearing with a bench, which Gabriel led me toward. I sat down beside him.

Even though I could hear laughter and happy chatter from the rest of the park and anyone could come around that corner any moment, it felt like we were alone among the walls of cornstalks.

I was just starting to get nervous about hiding from my family. Suddenly I heard my name.

As did everyone else at the Maize.

"Yael? Yael Lewis? This is your bat mitzvah calling!" Gabriel's dad's voice boomed out over the loudspeaker.

And then my friends chimed in, yelling in the maze, "Yael! Where are you?! It's time, it's time!"

I stood up.

"But wait," Gabriel said as he grabbed my hand to stop me from leaving. "You're bailing on the speech, right? That's why we're here."

I glanced past him toward the path we'd taken to get into the center of the maze, the one that I hoped I'd be able to follow out. "Uh . . ."

Gabriel pulled on my hand, bringing my attention back to him as he lifted an eyebrow. "You have to. You need to be your own girl."

I pointed at my shirt. "Uh, I'm a *woman* now,"

I said with an eye roll.

"Right," he said, smirking. "But still, you need to do what's in your heart, and if that means following your own path and not doing a speech that you don't want to do, then you belong right here." He nodded toward the bench beside him.

"YAEL? WHERE ARE YOU?" came out over the loudspeaker. This time it was my mom. And she sounded like she was none too pleased with the bat mitzvah girl.

"I have to go," I said, pulling my hand away from Gabriel's.

He snorted and shook his head. "I should have known you were a chicken."

My mouth dropped open. "I'm not a chicken," I said slowly, wishing I sounded a little more sure of it.

He just shrugged as he crossed his arms.

"Yael? Yael?" my friends chanted.

I had two seconds to decide if I wanted to skip my own party. Did I want to stay here with this boy who had just called me a chicken? Or did I want to go back into the barn where everyone I loved was waiting for me?

No. Brainer.

I turned away from Gabriel and stalked toward

(what I hoped was) the way out of the maze. Just before I turned the corner, I stopped and looked back at him. "You know what? I'm going to go back there and do my speech even though it's scary. And that's exactly what makes me *not* a chicken." I was shaking. "People are waiting on me. Of course I should be there. Running away is stupid."

He crossed his arms, smirked, and made a chicken sound: "Bak-bak."

Seriously? I straightened up. "You know what? You are less mature than my baby sister, and . . . and . . . I hope you get poop-bombed by a crow," I said before I turned away and started running blindly through the maze.

"The crows aren't even real!" Gabriel called after me, but I didn't care. I just wanted to get as far away from him as I could.

Which is when I got completely and totally lost.

I reached a junction with three options. "I'm never going to get out of here!" I yelled in frustration.

"Yael?" Tara! I whirled around.

"I'm lost!" I yelled to the cornflower-blue sky. "Where are you?"

"We're totally lost too!"

Ugh. Maybe the best way out was the most direct. I backed up and looked over the corn and could see the tip of the Ferris wheel. If I could just go toward that, I'd get out. But as I parted the corn, I was faced with a bigger problem than stalks of corn: chain-link fence.

"Oh no."

My phone buzzed in my pocket. I pulled it out to see a text string from my mom:

You did great today.

Where are you?

Everything okay?

Yael?

Getting worried! Txt me back!

So I did: I'm lost HELP!

Seconds later my phone rang.

"Mom?"

"Yael, where are you?" she said, sounding really concerned. "You're supposed to be in the barn!"

I had to swallow back the tears. "I know. I'm lost in the corn maze. I'm never going to get out . . . and . . ." I had to stop because all the air was going out of my lungs, and I was going to completely lose it. The last thing I wanted to do was have a Ranting Rivka–type tantrum.

"Yael, it's okay—I'll help you. Don't worry. I just pulled up the map of the maze on my cell. And with your GPS on your phone, I can walk you through."

"Oh! That's . . . Thank you!" I could have cried from relief, but instead I just straightened my shoulders and let my mom guide me.

.   .   .

I finally got out of the maze, and then a second later my friends erupted from a different path. We all hugged and laughed, relieved we wouldn't be stuck in the maze forever.

Realizing we were already late, I broke away, and we ran back to the barn. I wanted to use the bathroom and check my face, but before I could, my mom came barreling toward me and did that whole "I was SO worried about you!" dance, touching my face and looking in my eyes like I'd been lost in the woods for weeks, which it did feel like.

I hated that she was slobbering all over me, but I sort of loved it at the same time. Not that I'd ever tell her that.

"Mom!" I said, trying to get away from her because the way she was carrying on was starting to attract attention.

"Sorry, sorry," she said, tugging me over toward the stage. "I was getting worried, that's all. It's time for your speech. Are you ready?"

No, I wanted to say, but didn't. Because what my mother wouldn't understand was that I'd *never* be ready, but being a grown-up meant I would do what was right. That meant making a speech in front of all these people, no matter how scary.

I thought of the time when I'd been dying to try a new brush technique to give my painting movement, like what Emily Carr did in her painting *Edge of the Forest*. I had been worried I might ruin what I'd already painted if I couldn't get it just right. But I had to try to push myself, or I'd never improve as an artist.

This was just like that. I had to push myself. I had to try.

Just like Emily Carr had her own unique style to her paintings, I could do my speech my way. I could make my words be like my signature brushstrokes—and that meant it was okay if my speech was short and to the point. That was being true to myself.

I thanked my parents, grandparents, the rabbi, and all the guests. Then I looked over at my mom as I said, "And I especially need to thank my mom, because if it wasn't for her, I'd have had to make my speech from inside the corn maze."

That earned me a laugh and then it was over. Well, my speech was over. I sat back down as my dad took over the mic. He thanked everyone for coming and made his sweet dad speech—how proud he was of me, blah, blah, blah. I took a few deep, relieved breaths because the hard stuff was over; now I could just have fun.

As he went on, Eli came up beside me.

"You did an amazing job yesterday with your Torah portion and everything. And then just now with your speech."

I frowned at him. "I messed up my Torah portion yesterday."

He shrugged. "Only a little." It looked like he really meant it. "And seriously, who hasn't stumbled a bit over their reading? No one does a perfect job—remember the rabbi told us to just do our best? Your best was pretty darn good, Yael. And you barely looked nervous."

"Thanks, Eli," I said, giving him a smile. "That means a lot."

He leaned in close and whispered, "So, I guess there'll be dancing soon, huh?"

"Yeah," I said, glancing up at my dad, who was

still going on and on. "Someday."

He nodded and looked down at his shoes. "Cool. So, uh, will there be dancing?"

I looked at him. Was he asking me for a reason? Every bar or bat mitzvah we'd been to had dancing.

"Yeah," I said. "Why?"

He shrugged. "Maybe you'll want to dance with me?"

My heart thumped hard in my chest. Had he just asked me to dance? Eli Roth? I looked at him sideways to make sure he was serious. When he just looked back at me hopefully, I knew he was.

"Sure. That would be really cool."

Finally my dad finished his speech, and MC Mic took over the microphone. He called me out to the dance floor and asked what song I wanted for my first dance. I thought about it for a second and glanced at my friends. Then I saw Gabriel at the side of the stage, looking at me hopefully. I took a second to narrow my eyes at him before I leaned into the mic and declared, with as much confidence as I could muster, "The 'Chicken Dance'!"

After all, I was the bat mitzvah girl. Well, actually—I thought as I looked down at my shirt—the bat mitzvah *woman*. Once the music began, we all shrieked in excitement and headed out to the dance floor and started twisting and flapping. And laughing, of course.

Eli and I circled each other, flapping our "wings," having the time of our lives.

I looked around at the crowd, at everyone dancing and laughing—my classmates, my friends from shul, my family, even the Maize staff—everyone was having a great time.

Though there was no doubt in my mind that I was the happiest chicken in the barn.

As I danced over to my sister and picked her up so we could flap together, I realized she had been right. It really was the best bat mitzvah evah!

Still Life with Friends

All that stress and worry and planning for this one day, and it was finally here! Party time!

I still had to slog through a thank-you speech and suffer through my parents going on and on about me being a "woman," but the really hard stuff—performing my Torah portion in front of so many people—was behind me. Even I thought I'd done a good job at synagogue.

Before I had to do my speech, I would get to let loose with all my friends out in the amusement park and could almost relax. Hopefully, that would carry me through the stressful part.

My family arrived early, and once I was out of the car, I thanked each of my parents with a hug and sent them and Rivka off to the barn, where the party and dinner would be later. Then I stationed myself at the front gate, waiting for my friends to pull up in Paloma's van.

Ten long minutes later, they did.

"YAEL!!!" Tara hollered as she launched herself out of the van, pulling me into a crushing hug with one arm as she held out the other to take a selfie with her phone. "This will be the best day! We would have been here earlier, but we couldn't get Paloma's dad to drive any faster!"

"I was driving the speed limit," Mr. Garcia protested, leaning toward the open window. "Mazel tov, Yael."

"Thank you," I said, giving him a wave.

"Thanks, Dad!" Paloma yelled as she pulled the sliding door closed. "See you later."

She hugged me hard. I turned to Gemma to give her a hug too.

She was frowning at me and holding out her phone. "I wanted to capture you arriving."

Leave it to Gemma to think of everything.

"We can re-create it," Tara said, pointing toward the parking lot. "Yael, go over there and make it seem like you just got here. Be dramatic!"

Tara knew how to stage a scene. I did as she suggested, while Gemma propped her phone up on an unused ticket counter and started recording.

I grinned toothily as I walked from my parents' car to the booth to greet my favorite guests. Then we did the hugs again as if it were the first time, and I welcomed the girls (loudly, for the camera) to my bat mitzvah party.

"Aaaaaaaaand . . . scene!" Tara yelled.

Gemma pressed the stop button. "Perfect!"

We raced one another to the barn, whooping and laughing, to collect our wristbands so we could get on all the rides. We grabbed the T-shirts I'd made, the dark purple ones that had a robot wearing a *kippah* on the front.

As the four of us ducked into the bathroom to change into them, I felt a rush of pride because my friends couldn't stop gushing about how cool the shirts were.

When we emerged, I noticed Gabriel in the corner. I was about to point him out to my friends but remembered that this day was all about me and my best friends. No boy pressure.

We put on our wristbands and then headed out into the park.

· · ·

The bumper cars were closest to the barn, so that was where we stopped first.

It wasn't busy, so we went right up to the front and showed our wristbands. The guy running the ride gave us each a nod as he held the gate open. I stopped at the edge of the track and looked around, trying to decide which car to pick. Tara yelled my name and waved me over.

"This one!" she said. "It's your favorite, purple, *and* it has a thirteen on the back—it's a good-luck sign!"

"Awesome!" I said as we got into the car together.

"Have you ever driven before?" I asked her as I clicked the seat belt into place.

"Nope, but how hard can it be?" she said, reaching for the wheel.

I shrugged, and then she made a silly face at me and we both laughed. I looked over at the green car holding Paloma and Gemma and could tell by their determined looks that it was going to be an epic battle.

"Brace yourself," I said, pointing toward them.

"BRING IT ON!" Tara yelled at them.

We heard a chorus of whoops from the other

side, and we all looked to see Eli and Nick Parsons in another green car, Jin Lee and Ben Miller in a black one, and then next to them in a red one were Hiro Nakahara and Desmond Flynn.

"Forget Pal and Gem," Tara said. "We're going for the boys." She whistled at our friends and then nodded her head toward the cluster of boys' cars. Gemma and Paloma both nodded and tucked their chins. Time for war.

"Girl power!" Tara yelled, and we all pumped our fists in the air.

A bell rang out, signaling the ride was about to begin. We hollered and leaned on our horns.

And then it was go time.

"Oh, my abs, my abs!" I said, clutching my middle as we stumbled out of the cars.

As soon as the ride had powered up, we'd driven straight at Eli and Nick, slamming into them. We'd laughed so hard and had not stopped for the entire ride.

The more Tara had tried to ram the boys' cars, the worse a driver she became, and we'd spun off into the paths of other cars.

Tara couldn't speak. She just silently wiped laughter tears from her eyes.

"I am so ready for my license!" Gemma joked, high-fiving me as we all gathered outside the ride.

"You are a horrible driver," Eli said to Tara, but she was busy joking with Nick about his lack of driving skills and didn't hear him.

I shook my head at him. "Don't worry—it'll be years before she gets on a real road."

We joked a bit with the boys over who had landed the craziest hit before we left them to go into the bathroom to check our faces and hair.

"Ugh, I think I have whiplash," Paloma said, rubbing her neck.

Tara rolled her eyes. "Please. We hardly hit you."

"Uh-huh," Paloma said with a grin as she reached up to secure her ponytail. "That last time, you hit us head on, and I saw that look in your eye."

"What look?" Tara asked innocently. "I never gave a look."

"Sometimes," Gemma said teasingly, "you actually *aren't* the best actress."

"Ohhhhh, burn!" we all shouted at the mock insult.

"Come on," Tara said, linking her arm through mine. "Let's hit as many rides as we can before dinner."

We went to the Ferris wheel next. I almost chickened out when I saw Cam at the ticket counter. I *would* have chickened out if Tara hadn't put her arm around me and dragged me up to the line.

"Tara," I whispered. "No."

She squeezed me close, sensing I was about to bolt. "You can't avoid him forever. You've been dodging him since that day you faked sick."

"Yes, I know that," I bit out. After worrying my mother had told him about my horrible intestinal illness, I couldn't face him. Even the day before at synagogue, after I'd done my Torah portion, when he'd come up to congratulate me, I'd quickly thanked him and immediately turned to my aunt Shayla. I couldn't meet his eyes, I was so embarrassed.

I was *still* embarrassed. I would *forever* be embarrassed.

"Be brave," Tara growled as we got to the front.

"I *am*! Now let me go," I growled back, but it was no use; she was not letting me out of her grip.

"Hi, Cam," Tara said to him with a big smile, holding up her free hand and showing him her wristband.

"Hello, Tara, Yael, Paloma, and Gemma. Welcome to the Ferris wheel," he said, gesturing through the gate.

"How come you're stuck working during Yael's party?" Gemma asked.

"Someone called in sick today," Cam answered. "I'm just helping out. I'll still be able to attend the dinner."

"Hear that, Yael?" Tara stage-whispered.

I had and was relieved, but ignored her.

Cam seemed to also. "Enjoy your ride," he said. "Two to a car, please."

I was terrified he was going to bring up my "illness," since he seemed to always say what he thought—Tara had said before that he had no filter, and she was right.

But he didn't say anything about it, thankfully. Whew! Maybe my mom hadn't told him the details.

We didn't even need to discuss seating arrangements as we went into the ride enclosure—of course it was Tara and me in one car and Paloma and Gemma in another. Tara and I went first and got in the car at the bottom of the wheel, then we went up a bit at a time as each car filled up with people. Finally, when the entire ride was full, the wheel went around and around, showing us a view of Knot's Valley that I'd never seen before.

"That's so cool," I said, looking out over the valley, almost able to pick out my house. "Can you see your house?" I asked Tara, but when she didn't answer, I looked over at her.

She was looking down at the ground.

I nudged her with my elbow. "What are you looking at?"

She lifted her head and looked at me, seeming surprised. "Cam."

I glanced down. I felt a little woozy. From the height, of course. Cam was standing at the bottom of the ride, taking tickets. "What do you mean?"

"He keeps looking up at us as we go around. At *you*, actually. I think he likes you."

My mouth went dry, but I swallowed and said, "He isn't and he doesn't. You watch too many silly romances, Tara."

She rolled her eyes. "Whatever."

I couldn't help myself. I looked down again. Sure enough, Cam's head was angled back, and he was looking up. I couldn't know for sure that he was looking at me, but he seemed to be tracking our car as we went up and up to the top of the wheel's arc. . . . Could he be looking at me?

"CAM!" Tara suddenly yelled out as she waved her arms. Now he was *definitely* looking at us.

"What are you doing?" I demanded frantically, and grabbed on to the bar because the car was swinging thanks to her waving.

Then my best friend hollered, for all of Knot's Valley to hear, "YAEL SAYS HI!"

I closed my eyes. "You didn't just do that."

I heard Paloma and Gemma whoop and whistle.

But then I heard Cam's voice float up. "Hi, Yael! I hope you're having a wonderful ride!"

My eyes flew open. *What?*

I looked down then, thankful that if I couldn't quite tell if he was smiling from this distance, he probably couldn't see how hard I was blushing. I *could* see that he was waving up at us as we started down on the other side of the wheel.

"Wave back, silly," Tara said as she leaned her shoulder into mine.

I did, and as we got closer and closer to the ground, I could see that Cam was looking right at me. And smiling.

• • •

After the Ferris wheel we went into the park's famous corn maze. I didn't have a great sense of direction and was sure I'd get lost, so I was glad to be with Paloma, a gamer who played a ton of simulation games and assured us she'd have no trouble finding the way out.

Tara wanted us to compete—two against two—to get to the middle, but I said I wanted the four of us to stay together. Mostly to keep Paloma and her navigation skills close, but also because these were my friends and this day was about the four of us. We ran through the maze, laughing as we turned corners and tried to scare one another. It was a little spooky in the maze as the sun began to set and the crickets started to chirp. There were even some creepy stuffed crows peeking out at us from between the really tall stalks of corn.

Speakers pumped out weird music that made it harder to figure out where we were because, between the music and the *whoosh-whoosh* of the cornstalks, we could barely hear sounds from the rest of the park.

We found the middle of the maze, where there was a bench and a scarecrow holding a sign congratulating us for finding the center. We took a bunch of selfies and then had this random kid take a picture of the four of us with the scarecrow.

"Well, this has been fun, but I should probably look over my speech one more time," I said. "Let's head back."

We looked at Paloma.

She bit her lip as she looked at the three paths before us. "Ummm . . ."

After what felt like hours of searching, we ended up back in the center. "I guess I'll have my fourteenth birthday here too. And fifteenth and sixteenth and . . ."

Nobody laughed. We were tired and hungry. And it was getting darker.

We sat on the bench in glum silence until I got an idea. I pulled out my phone and opened a text.

Hi Cam, we're stuck in the middle of the corn maze! Help!

I thought he would send me directions, since he was busy working, but he quickly responded: Dear Yael, stay in the center and I will come find you. Sincerely, Cam Thompson

I sighed in relief and showed the screen to my friends, who cheered. Only a few minutes later

Cam turned the corner into the center of the maze (Gemma, who was ready, snapped a photo of the event).

"Thank you so much for saving us, Cam," Tara said. "Yael is SOOOOOOO thankful, aren't you, Yael?"

I reached over to pinch her, but she scurried behind Cam, who frowned in confusion. "Thanks, Cam," I said. "It's almost time to head into the barn for dinner and the dance party."

Cam nodded. "I'm looking forward to that."

I followed him as he turned down a path. "You are?" I asked.

"Yes," he said. "I'm quite hungry."

Oh. Right.

As if on cue, my own stomach grumbled. "Excuse me!" I said, pressing a palm over my noisy belly.

Cam smiled. "Looks like I saved you just in time."

"We were going to start eating the corn," Gemma said.

"Good luck with that," Cam said. "It's decorative corn—not very tasty."

"We could have died in here!" Tara said dramatically.

"Hardly," Paloma said in a pouty voice. "I would have gotten us out. Eventually."

I rolled my eyes at that.

"I know the way out by heart now," Cam said. "But it's easy to navigate; you just need to know to look for the crows."

"The crows?"

"Yes," he said. "Their beaks point toward the exit."

"What?" I looked for one of the birds, and when I did, I noticed my friends were walking a little way behind us.

Tara smirked at me. It was no accident that they were giving Cam and me space. I turned back to follow Cam.

"Yes," Cam went on. "See? Here's one at a fork, and his beak is pointing to the right. That is the path to get out."

"That's so clever," I said.

He nodded and then after a few more turns (where I noticed all the crows) he said, "So, speaking of eating . . ."

"Yeah?" I said warily, not having any idea what he was about to say.

He cleared his throat. "Maybe on Tuesday when we go back to school, we can eat lunch together."

Whoa.

I looked over my shoulder, and all three of my besties had wide eyes and were nodding. Gemma had her thumbs up, but then Tara waved toward Cam's back, reminding me that he was probably expecting me to say something.

Urk! "Uh, yeah, that would be cool, Cam. I'd love to."

He smiled at me as we got to the entrance of the maze. "Great. I have to run back to the Ferris wheel to help my uncle lock it down, but I'll see you inside at your party."

"Awesome, thanks again for your help," I said.

"You're welcome."

And then he was gone.

My friends gathered around me, and we did a big group hug as we all squealed in excitement.

"This is the best bat mitzvah ever!" Tara said. I didn't point out that it was the only bat mitzvah she'd been to, but she was absolutely right.

Broad Strokes

At the barn I immediately looked around for
Cam. The dancing wouldn't be until after dinner,
but I wanted to make sure I knew where he was
at all times. I'd helped my mother create the seating chart, so I knew he was supposed to be at
table seven, but so far it was just a few kids from
his class there.

I checked around backstage, but he wasn't
there, nor was he in the hall by the bathrooms. I
was going to try the kitchen, but as I approached,
it sounded so busy that I didn't want to get in
anyone's way.

I gave up and went to the head table to join my family as other people drifted into the barn and took their seats. I'd wanted to sit with my friends, but my mom said that sitting with family was "non-negotiable." When Dad had shaken his head at me as I'd opened my mouth to argue, I knew she meant it, so I didn't bother.

I sat down and decided to take a couple of minutes while everyone settled at their tables to go over my speech. I reached into my back pocket and gasped: It was gone! Not even a trace of pocket lint. I looked around the table and the floor but didn't see it. It could be anywhere!

Oh no! Cue panic mode. I hadn't memorized it or put it on my phone or anything. My brain was like a blank canvas, and I had no paint. What was I supposed to do now?

I looked up to see if I could find my mom in the crowd and saw her with the caterer, but before I could catch her eye, the two of them disappeared into the kitchen. My dad was way over on the other side of the barn, talking to my great-aunt Ruthie, Rivka at his side, tugging on his hand insistently.

I just sat there, frozen and fighting back tears, watching as my sister finally broke away from Dad. He turned from Aunt Ruthie and called her name, but she pointed toward me. "Yael!"

Dad caught my eye questioningly, and I nodded. If she was about to have a tantrum, I may as well join her.

She came right up to me and crawled into my lap. "Yael, the bat mizvah girl!" she said, and even considering my mood, I couldn't help but smile at her. She was wearing one of my bat mitzvah shirts, tied up into a cute knot by her hip to make it into something of a dress over her tights.

"Hiya, Rivvy," I said, not meaning to sound so dejected, but unable to help it.

She frowned. "What's a matter?"

"I lost my speech."

She looked around, though I'm not sure she even knew what she was looking for. "The paper I wrote my speech on," I clarified. "It's gone. I lost it out in the park somewhere, and now I don't know what to say when I have to get up in front of everyone. This is turning into the worst bat mitzvah ever."

My sister stared at me, and then half a second later her chin began to wobble. And her lip started to quiver. Then her eyes filled with tears.

Nooooooo!!!!!! Backtrack, Yael, or you're going to be really sorry in about two seconds!

"Rivvy, Rivvy," I said quickly, giving her a reassuring hug. "It's okay, don't cry!"

"But, but . . ." She took in a shuddering breath like she was priming her lungs to let loose. "Worst ba' mizvah! You said 'WORST BA' MIZVAH!'"

"No," I said, forcing myself to smile VERY WIDELY. I probably looked like a lunatic. "I didn't mean it. I was just kidding. I will do my speech no problem. I just have to make sure I thank Mom and Dad and the rabbi and remember that everyone here loves me and wants to see me do a good job. It'll be fine—all part of being a grown-up."

One lone tear escaped Rivka's right eye, but as I wiped it from her cheek, the quiver went away and the wobble slowed down.

Whew!

One problem solved. Just not the big one.

Several minutes later, after Mom returned from the kitchen and Rivka ran off to join her, I was still sitting there, trying to rebuild my speech in my head. I'd sort of convinced myself that what I'd said to Rivka was true—that I could wing the speech and it would be fine—but not entirely.

"Is something wrong?" Cam said as he came up beside me.

I took a deep breath and said, "I lost my speech and I never memorized it, so now I'm struggling with figuring out what I should say."

Cam gave me a nod before he turned around and walked away.

Oh. Okay then.

I touched my fingers to the corners of my eyes, mopping up sudden tears, feeling so stupid.

I spent the next two minutes trying to convince myself that no one would think it was strange if I just thanked my parents and the rabbi and said it was dinnertime. Short and sweet.

But then, several moments of feeling sorry for my doomed, speechless self later, Cam returned holding a piece of paper. I jumped out of my seat because I thought he'd found my speech, but then my heart sank when I realized the paper looked all wrong—it was pale yellow, and my speech had been printed on regular white paper.

"What's that?" I asked as he came close and held out the page toward me.

"Your speech."

I sighed. "No it isn't."

"Oh," he said. "I don't mean it's the exact one you lost. I mean I wrote it down."

Glancing up from the paper to his eyes, I asked, "What?"

"I wrote it down for you," he said again, pushing the paper toward me. "I read it before, remember?"

I took the page from him and started reading his very precise printing. It really *was* my speech!

"How did you do that?!"

"I have an excellent memory," Cam said. He wasn't bragging, either, just stating a fact.

I shouldn't have been surprised, since I already knew he was super smart, but I didn't realize he had such an amazing memory, too. "Cam! Thank you!" I said, feeling weird, like I should hug him or something.

"You're welcome," he said with a tiny smile, and then turned and walked away from me without saying anything else. I realized it was just his way as I watched him go, grinning because today had reminded me why I liked him.

I did it!

Sure, I said a billion "ums" and didn't look up once during my speech, but everyone laughed at the parts they were supposed to laugh at, and during it I heard, "That's right, Yael!" and "Hear,

hear, Yael!" I got to tell everyone that my parents were the best grown-ups I knew—which was the most important thing. Everyone actually applauded when I was done and not just because it was time to eat!

Thank you for saving me, Cam Thompson!

After dinner and a bit of fast dancing, a slow song came on, and while I looked out for Cam, he was nowhere to be seen. But then I sensed someone tall beside me. I swiveled around, a huge smile on my face to greet Cam.

It wasn't Cam.

"Hey, bat mitzvah girl," Gabriel said, his face all smug and obnoxious. "Do I get my dance now?"

I opened my mouth to tell him no thanks, but then Cam *was* there, asking me if I wanted to join him on the Ferris Wheel.

"Hi, Cam," I said, emphasizing his name. "Yep, let's go."

As I left the barn with him, I heard Tara say something to Gabriel about wishing a house fell on him. One more reason to love that girl.

Cam didn't say anything for the whole walk, all the way to the Ferris wheel. When we got there, he greeted Fred, the guy who ran the ride, and leaned in to say something to him. Fred glanced at me and then smiled back at Cam, giving him a nod.

We stepped into the car and took our seats before Cam pulled the bar across us, checking it three times. As we waited for the ride to start, he told me the history of the Ferris wheel—not the one we were on, but the first one, built by some guy (whose last name was, unsurprisingly, Ferris) in Chicago.

While I wasn't really interested in the history, I liked that he was talking, because it meant I didn't have to. Not only was I getting nervous because of how high we were going, but we were alone, and I wasn't entirely sure why he'd wanted to bring me on the ride.

I *thought* he liked me, but that didn't mean I knew what to expect. Especially from Cam, who could be very random and unpredictable.

We had to wait for the other people to get on the other cars, making us rise up and up by increments.

Finally, we were at the top, and I gasped as I realized we could see out to what seemed like the end of the earth. The sun was beginning to set, lighting up the sky with orange, pink, and purple streaks. It was like a stunning watercolor, and I tried to capture it in my memory so I could paint it later.

We could still hear shouts and laughs from people on other rides, but the sounds seemed really far away, and it was as though we were in another world.

"It's nice up here, huh?" Cam asked, his voice softer than usual.

I looked over at him and noticed he seemed more relaxed, even though we were nerve-rackingly high up in the air. "Yeah. It's like a fairyland or something."

"That's why I like it up here. I can hear myself think without a million sounds competing for my brain. And I like seeing the sunset and the way it reflects off the clouds."

"It's really pretty."

He smiled at me. "I can see the lights reflected off your glasses. It looks like you have rainbows for eyes."

Okaaaaay. He was so weird. As confusing—and interesting—as an Escher sketch.

"I like you, Yael. Thank you for inviting me to your bat mitzvah."

"You're welcome," I said, not pointing out the

fact that I'd invited the entire eighth grade. "And, uh, I like you, too."

Masterpiece

Inside the barn, I immediately looked around for Eli. I hadn't seen him for most of the party, and that made me feel bad. I finally spotted him near the head table, talking with my mother.

I walked up to them, mostly to save him from my mom, though he didn't seem to mind chatting with her. They both abruptly stopped talking as I approached.

"Oh, hey," Eli said. "Having a good time?"

"The best," I said, not looking at him and wondering what to do with my hands. Why was this so awkward? I've known Eli forever!

"Welcome back, everyone!" Micah boomed into the microphone, breaking through my thoughts. "We're going to start dinner, so please take your seats."

Thankful for the interruption, I hurried up to the head table and sank into my chair, realizing I'd been a little rude to Eli.

I peeked at him as he walked over to table seven and sat with the rest of my friends. He said something, and they all burst out laughing. I wished I could hear what they were saying.

Tara caught my eye, wagged her eyebrows, and nodded toward Eli. I rolled my eyes back at her, hoping my friends weren't going to say anything embarrassing about me to him. Since Paloma had said she was rooting for Eli, I was suspicious.

I watched as Tara leaned across Paloma, who was between them, and said something to Eli that made him straighten in his chair. His eyes flicked to me but then quickly returned to Tara. He said something to her, making her eyes go wide before her head swiveled toward me.

I lifted my eyebrows at her, but her lips spread into a very wicked grin.

What are you up to, Tara Singh?

She said something more to Eli, and then *he* looked up at me! My heart was thumping hard now, as his eyes widened and Paloma's mouth stretched into a big smile. My two terrible, awful, meddling best friends very pointedly looked right at me.

"Mazel tov. Enjoy your dinner." A waiter appeared at my side, breaking into my thoughts as he set down a huge plate of food in front of me.

Too bad I wasn't hungry anymore.

Do you want to dance?

Hey, let's dance!

Eli Roth, would you do me the honor of...

I was eating the last bite of my cake, considering (and rejecting) all the ways to ask Eli to dance, when my mother pushed back her chair and went up to the podium that had been set up next to the head table. She adjusted the microphone and smiled out at everyone as the buzz of conversation died down. "I hope everyone is enjoying their dessert. As you finish up and before we get to the music and dancing part of the evening, we have a few speeches."

I took a deep breath to calm my suddenly jumping nerves, even though I knew I still had time. My parents wanted to say some things, and then I would go after them. But as I glanced over at my dad, he was still eating and wasn't moving to get up from his seat. Had they changed the plan? Was I next? I put my fork down. My mouth suddenly felt chalky. Mom looked out at table seven and smiled as she waved toward my friends.

As I tried to figure out what was going on, Eli got up out of his chair.

What is happening? Because for some reason, Eli was walking up to the podium. His face was a little red, but he was smiling.

Mom leaned into the microphone and said, "Yael's friends, Eli Roth and Tara Singh, asked if they could say a few words."

As I watched, dumbstruck, Eli hugged my mom and took her place at the podium, looking out over the sea of tables. Then he turned his head and looked at me. Right at me. I could feel every head in the barn swivel toward me, all eyes focused on me like lasers. I swallowed.

"Hi," he and Tara said in unison.

"Hi?" I replied automatically. My heart was thumping so loudly I could barely hear myself speak.

"I hope you don't mind?" It was like Eli was talking to just me, while the hushed crowd looked on.

I shrugged and waved toward the podium. "It's . . ." I cleared my throat. "No, it's okay."

He nodded and turned toward the microphone. "I've known Yael for a very long time—ever since I was young. . . ." He paused while a bunch of people laughed. "And while I know we're all super proud of her for the great job with her Torah portion yesterday . . ." He paused again while people clapped. "Tara and I wanted to share why we're proud of her and proud to know her. There is a side to Yael that not everyone knows."

What? Panic washed over me as I stared at him.

Tara looked at me and smiled before she said, "Yael is not the type of girl to brag about all the great things she can do, so I thought I would do that on her behalf. Actually, I thought I'd show you."

WHAT. IS. HAPPENING?

The lights went out, and a hush fell over the crowd. A screen slowly dropped down from the ceiling with a *whirrrrr* that seemed deafening in the silent barn. Even Rivka was quiet!

Were they going to show baby pictures of me? Or photos of that time we gave each other haircuts?

Please let this not be either of those things.

The projector switched on.

But then—I couldn't believe it—*my* artwork flashed across the screen. From some of my earliest (and embarrassing) pieces, like the tissue-paper collage of the tree in Eli's backyard and the sketch of his dog, Pepper (I couldn't believe he'd kept it), to some recent ones. Good ones, like the charcoal of the night sky that I'd made for Tara, a watercolor of the lake at camp, and even my latest self-portrait. I was really proud of that one, especially when Dad had taken it to work and hung it in his office. Which meant my parents must have supplied pictures of the artwork to Eli and Tara.

I felt my entire face get hot and was grateful for the dim lighting, but then I looked out at the crowd: Everyone was smiling. My older cousin had a hand to her mouth, her eyes wide in awe. My classmates didn't look bored, their eyes trained on the screen. My friends, well, they looked so proud and impressed that my flush turned into a warm feeling of happiness.

As the slideshow continued, Eli went on. "Yael was called to the Torah yesterday, but her *true* calling is art. Yael expresses herself through her creations, and I think you'd all agree that she's really talented."

Murmurs went up through the crowd, and there was a lot of nodding.

I looked over at Mom and Dad to see them beaming. I leaned toward Dad and asked quietly, "Whose idea was this?"

He nodded toward Eli, who was now talking about the time I'd had him pose like a superhero for a painting and how his muscles had completely seized up the next day. "All his," Dad said as he looked at me, his eyes glossy in the light from the projector. "For people who are so completely uncreative, we are so proud to have created you, Yael."

"Thanks, Dad," I said, leaning in to wrap my arms around his shoulders. I looked at the amazing party my mother had planned for me and remembered the clever ways my dad had mediated our family fights. I wouldn't say they were *completely* uncreative. "We're not the only ones who know it either," Dad added. He lifted his right eyebrow and nodded toward Eli again.

"Daaaaaad," I said. But I wasn't really annoyed. And then an even better thing happened.

When the slideshow ended, Tara turned to me and, as though there were no one else in the room, said, "You make everything colorful, Yael. Even bat mitzvahs."

Everyone raised their glasses of champagne or sparkling apple juice.

"Hear, hear! To Yael!" they toasted.

After the clinking of glasses was done and I was able to catch my breath (sort of), Eli walked over and said, "Do you want to dance?"

"What about *my* speech?" I squeaked out, and then turned to look at my mom.

She had a goofy smile on her face, which made sense since she'd been in on this whole scheme. "It can wait. Go have fun."

Just then a slow song came on—Chumz's latest—and a squeal erupted from table seven. My heart started to thump hard because—

"Yael . . ."

I startled and turned my head toward the voice. Eli was standing a few feet away, looking at me, his hands in his pockets. I got up out of my chair and took the few steps that brought me to him.

"Thank you," I said. He gave me one of his big smiles and nodded toward the back of the barn.

I fell in step beside him as all around us people were chatting and slowly—or, in the case of my friends, quickly—making their way onto the dance floor. It made me laugh to think that I had spent so much energy trying to figure out how to ask him to dance when all this time he was planning the same thing.

"Why are you laughing?" he asked.

"Because it's funny how things work out," I said. "I . . . I'm glad you're here, Eli."

"Me too, Yael," he replied as we found ourselves in a quiet corner of the barn, where hay bales were stacked in a pyramid.

In sync, we sat down on a hay bale and watched the dancers.

I took a big breath and looked at him. "Thanks for everything," I said. "Your presentation . . . That was really cool."

He smiled at me. "You're welcome. I wanted to do something special for you."

I snorted, not bothering to cover it up because this was Eli—he'd heard me snort a million times. "That was special, all right!"

"Good," he said with a nod. He looked down

at his feet. "I wanted *you* to feel special, Yael."
Then he paused, and it was just about to get
weird when he looked up at me and said, "Not all
stars are in the sky, you know."

I turned my whole body toward him and, in
the multicolored disco lights, looked at my oldest
friend. He was the same old Eli . . . but also not.
"Thanks," I said softly.

"Also . . . ," he said, his cheeks getting all
pink—and not just from the lights—as he darted
his eyes anywhere but at me. "Um . . ."

What was he hiding? "Did you do something
else?"

"Noooooo," he said, and ran his fingers
through his mop of hair before he finally blurted it
out. "Just . . . well, I've heard that the guy you dance
with first at your bat mitzvah is your boyfriend."

TARA! I glanced at the dance floor at my
best friend, who was, of course, in the middle
of a circle of people all clapping for her and
her dance partner—my seventy-two-year-old
great-uncle Chaim.

I shook my head and turned back to Eli, who
was biting his lip, looking at me expectantly.

"I've heard that too," I said with a laugh. "I'm
pretty sure it's some sort of law or something."

"Exactly," he said, and then raised his eyebrows and asked, "You're okay with that law?"

"Very okay," I said.

I stood up, took his hand, and pulled him to the dance floor.